SPLICE
The Novelization

CLAIRE DONNER

Based on the screenplay by
VINCENZO NATALI
ANTIONETTE TERRY BRYANT
and DOUG TAYLOR

Encyclopocalypse Publications
www.encyclopocalypse.com

Copyright © 2009 by Vincenzo Natali
All Rights Reserved.

ISBN: 978-1-960721-45-7

Cover Artwork by Stephen Imhoff
Cover Layout by Sean Duregger
Interior design and formatting by Sean Duregger

The characters and events in this book are fictitious. Any similarity to real persons, living, dead or undead is coincidental and not intended by the author.

No part of this book may be reproduced in any form or by any electronic or mechanical means, including information storage and retrieval systems, without permission in writing from the publisher, except by a reviewer who may quote brief passages in a review.

FOREWORD

VINCENZO NATALI

The genesis of SPLICE began with a mouse, all-be-it a very special mouse. The Vacanti Mouse, as it was known, appeared to have a human ear growing out of its back. In reality scientists had implanted artificial ear cartilage beneath its skin to see if it would be rejected by the mouse's immune system. Beyond the outward surreality of the mouse what struck me was how vulnerable it looked. It was hairless... naked, and didn't seem happy to be the host for this alien appendage. I intuited that there was a movie in the mouse. Something in the intersection between the irrationality of human nature and the power of genetic science.

SPLICE's first incarnation was a short film that I wrote with Antionette Terry-Bryant while in film school together. But the potential of the story seemed to want more screen time. And so we crafted a feature film script. I remember that we finished it on Valentine's Day 1998. You could call that the moment of conception. But it would take another twelve years of gestation and the collaboration of one more writer, Doug Taylor, before our baby was fully formed.

SPLICE was never going to have an easy birth because among other things it explored the sexual desires that are shared between the creators and their creation. It was designed to tread transgressive terrain. Over the years various studios and producers were tempted by the possibilities, but ultimately too afraid to commit. In early 2000 I got very close to actually making it, but after I spent a year prepping it, the plug was pulled. The result was that not only was the film cancelled but it now had the additional burden of the five hundred thousand dollars spent in prep owed to the original producer.

At that point, I assumed it was dead. I kept waiting to read the announcement that someone else was going to make a genetic Frankenstein movie (an idea that seemed so obvious to me that I was sure it would happen), but as the years went by for some strange reason such a thing never materialized. And then one day, my producing partner, Steve Hoban, asked to look at the original contracts. He discovered that the money was not owed until principal photography, meaning SPLICE could be optioned at anytime by anyone for no additional cost. Then by coincidence I was contacted by a French producer friend, Yves Chevalier, who had just taken a post at the venerable French film studio, Gaumont, and was looking for projects. And then another planet aligned, I met Guillermo Del Toro and Don Murphy both of whom wanted to support the film. Suddenly, with the confluence of these entities there was the desire and the means to make SPLICE.

Like Dren, the creature at the center of the story, who has a penchant at the edge of death to return to life stronger than before, our film went into production within the year. This pattern repeated itself through out SPLICE's production and post-production. It would reach a point of near-disaster, only for a confluence of circumstances to then rescue it and provide us with an outcome that was better than was expected. Even after the film was finished, it was in danger of never being seen outside of a video store. The 2008 world wide financial meltdown had made it almost impossible to sell a movie, especially an expensive one like ours to an American distributor. Our original distributor had gone out of business while we were in post. At that point the only interest we got was from MGM, but then they also went bankrupt. Fortunately, we were accepted to the Sundance film festival where Joel Silver, the famous producer of the Lethal Weapon, Die Hard and Matrix films, saw SPLICE and wanted to acquire it for Dark Castle, his shingle at Warner Brothers. Miraculously, our weird indie horror film ended up with a two thousand theatre release from a major Hollywood studio in the summer of 2010. Unbelievable.

Unfortunately, SPLICE did not succeed in its initial theatrical release. But still *it would not die*. Over the years its popularity grew, and as recently as last year it became a surprise hit when it appeared on Netflix, and to my delight, inspired a wave of shock, disgust and glee on social media from a new generation of viewers. Something in the DNA of the film has remained potent, and like a child that has grown up to lead an exciting life after leaving its parents, I have had the pleasure of watching SPLICE wend its way into the popular consciousness.

The latest incarnation of this phenomenon is the book that you hold in your hands. Never in my wildest imaginings would I have expected that nearly fifteen years after finishing the movie there would be a published novelization. But what makes this an especially delicious event is that Claire Donner has found a way to imbue the text with a depth and complexity that in some ways goes beyond the film. Much like Dren, this novel is more than the sum of its parts. She has brought a psychological depth that combined with her unique prose, which is at once clinical and poetic, perfectly expresses the duality of the human heart that beats beneath the science.

Reading this book for the first time, I was reminded of the archetypes that belie the contemporary narrative. Dren is mythical in her conception, to borrow the oft used Greek term, a *chimera*, who has in some fashion patiently waited for our technology to awaken her from the depths of our subconscious and manifest her in the material world. The parts of the book that I find especially poignant are those that take her point of view. At last, Dren's inner world is given a voice that the medium of film could never grant her.

Most of all, I enjoy that Claire has affection for all the players in this tragedy, and is willing attribute positive and negative traits to all parties. She paints in shades of grey and digs deep into the mechanics of this complex and thoroughly bizarre love triangle. In doing so she fulfills my greatest hope for SPLICE—that it would pick up the baton from Mary Shelley's FRANKENSTEIN and carry it into the new Millennium. Her take on the Promethean myth has only grown in relevance and I have no doubt that some iteration of it will come to pass in the real world… perhaps before too long.

While we wait for that to happen, sit back and enjoy this wonderful rendition, which far exceeds the expectations of a 'novelization' and is unto itself a entirely independent and self-actualized creation.

Vincenzo Natali, January 2024

SPLICE
The Novelization

SHE IS NOT SUPPOSED TO EXIST

1

In the beginning, there was nothing. Or rather, there was everything. An infinite continuum of unexpressed potential. As bright as it was dark. As warm as it was cool. As close as it was vast. So full of possibility as to neutralize all distinctions. There was no inside, no outside. No this, no that. If there was a sound —say, the regular sluicing of fluid, or the hum of electricity—it was so constant as to be imperceptible, a non-sound. There was no hunger, as every want was preemptively quenched. There was no loneliness, as there was no individuation: No you, no me, no friend or foe. There was only an endless, unbroken, all-embracing consciousness from which escape, exteriority, and opposition were unthinkable. A beautiful, frictionless monotony where the division of before and after, thought and action, pain and pleasure, was inconceivable, unnecessary, without mean- ing. It was eternal peace. Wholeness. Grace. There was only Being.

And then, there came change. First, there was *movement*. A shifting, jarring interruption of the Being's perfect equilibrium. An arrhythmic jostling that created a disorienting feeling of back and forth, of up and down. This meant there was space, and if there was motion through space, then that meant the

Being had boundaries; it was somewhere and not elsewhere, it had a beginning and end, a fore and aft, an interior and exterior. It was singular. There was itself, and there was everything else.

Next, there came *sound*. A burbling, sucking, flushing noise. A shrill beeping and a low, heavy chugging whose rhythm described an on-ness and an off-ness, a then and a now, substance and void, something and nothing. More sounds brought more confusion, coming in random, clustered spikes: piercing clanks, blunt clicks and pops, a rending, a slicing, and something softer around the edges, almost musical that chattered, murmured, grunted, or rose suddenly in sharp little cries. The Being had only just accepted its own distinctions, its own inside and outside, its being here and not there, and now it faced the frightening fact that there were more beings out there beyond its own boundaries. Others. Beings perhaps like itself, perhaps not.

It would find out soon enough, once there came *light*, asserting its difference from dark, it gave shape to these Others. The revelations of the light inflicted on the Being an annihilating fear—a feeling that was itself something new, something that had no place in the fathomless stasis of before. The stark terror of individuation, of opposition, of self and other, thrust the memory of grace forever into the past—the before state— leaving the Being shivering and naked in the appalling new after. It was almost grateful for the unsettling warmth of the grasping extremities that wrapped themselves around the Being and drew it toward the Others.

"OK, I can see him. That's it, here he comes!"

Then came the first sensation. It was *pain*: that most informative of feelings. The Others, many times the Being's size, had breached its container, which suddenly seemed quite small and not at all like an endless field of soothing sameness. They lifted its body from the nutritious ooze in which it had no memory of forming. As this protective slime sloughed away, the Being was struck by the *cold*, a brutal attack that brought on an agonizing awareness of the limits of its soft, weak skin.

"Careful!"

"Alright, I got him, I got him."

"Vitals?"

"Stable."

The gargantuan Others hoisted the Being into the frigid air, and in that shocking moment it became aware of *smells*. A pungent odor came from its captors, an invisible effluvium rasping in and out of some unseen orifices; something warm and alive, but with an undercurrent of musky rot, simultaneously attractive and repulsive. There was something else, too, that didn't come from the Others themselves, but that was all around them. A death smell. Not death as in decay, but as in the opposite of life. This desiccating, cold-burning aroma clung to the sharp, glinting objects the *Others* used to sever the tie between the Being and the visceral sac that once fed it.

"Severing umbilical. OK, umbilical's cut. Clear."

Too much. All too much. The Being's consciousness began to retreat from the onslaught of newness. Its perceptions were swallowed up mercifully by an onrushing darkness that closed in around it. The sounds grew louder, as if they could hold the Being in place, but none could find purchase in its consciousness as it slid back toward a deep, primordial, hopefully eternal slumber.

"Wait! BP's dropping fast."

"Respirations are slow, shallow, and irregular."

"O2 sat's down 82%."

"BP 80 over 30. He's in V-tach."

"Get the paddles!"

"May have I some dopamine, please?"

Then: *a pinprick*. The sensitive outer membrane of the Being was punctured, the violation announced by an unprecedented agony.

Then: *a shock*. Jarring, convulsive, abject violence.

It all came flooding back. Heat. Cold. Alarming cacophonies and macabre smells. Blazing light and blinding shadow. And these alien Others who towered over the Being and manipulated it as they pleased. The teachers of the first and most important lesson about the World into which they had delivered it, a lesson that all must learn or perish: the knowledge of pain and its origins. To avoid the punishing proclamations of pain, one must know where it comes from.

Pain comes from difference.

"Heart rate's stable."

"Easy, easy."

"OK, we're good."

Holding the shivering creature in her gloved palms, Elsa Kast kept him level as she walked, swiftly but smoothly, toward the incubator—a technique she learned while waitressing her way through school, never imagining that the cafe and the clinic would have so much crossover. Once she lowered the fleshy little blob into his new home, Clive Nicoli closed the lid. The incubator sealed itself off with a soft sucking sound. They finally had a clear view of the newborn as it warmed up under the heat lamps, like a chick in a children's class project. With a sigh of relief, Clive and Elsa lowered their surgical masks.

"No physical discrepancies."

"He's perfect. He's just...*perfect*."

Elsa noted a tremor in her partner's voice, but there was no time to sit back and admire their work. They wheeled the incubator out of the birthing chamber and into the clean room next door, where they parked it between a pair of softly glowing UV panels. The light illuminated a group of anxious faces crowding the window of the observation room, greedy for a glimpse of the new arrival. Now came the real test.

"I like 'Melvin'. He's much more of a Melvin," Clive joked dryly to ease their suspense.

Elsa knew what he was going to say before it came out of his mouth. Clive had already pitched the idea of calling all their test subjects "Melvin", after a snooty experimental rock band he favored. Elsa retorted that this was not a useful naming convention, which Clive surely knew, but he was a habitual name-dropper—and the nerdier the reference, the better. He was always eager to let people know what he knew. Elsa was… rather the opposite.

"Somehow, Ginger and *Melvin* don't have quite the same ring to it."

"OK then, 'Fred' it is."

With the doors to the clean room sealed behind them, Clive took the little monster off the incubator and headed for a large glass tank on a platform in the center of the room. This enclosure, open at the top, could have accommodated a pair of over-sized guinea pigs; at the far end of the otherwise empty space, a set of small steel dishes of nutritive paste and potable water were lined up against a frosted plastic hut. Against its semi-translucent wall, one could see the shadow of something shivering inside. Elsa picked up a camcorder and circled the tank, positioning herself for a prime view of what came next. This part was nearly as perilous as the delivery itself, but if it went well, her recording would be an important reference document for years to come. Perhaps even a classic.

Fred squirmed in Clive's arms, responding to his father's warmth. "Alright…come on, little fella."

Finally, Elsa cracked a smile, scrunching up her nose in a way that Clive had always found particularly fetching. "He's so *cute!*"

Elsa had a bit of an ice queen thing going on, and Clive melted whenever she broke character, even if what moved her was a little mysterious. The creature in Elsa's monitor was a wrinkled loaf of Caucasoid flesh around the size of a football, along whose surface one could see a gray network of softly pulsing blood vessels. Fred had no discernible facial features and appeared less like a fully formed animal than a lambskin sack with an animal wiggling inside of it. His lumpy, bulbous rear end anchored a long muscular trunk, and a pair of oblong lobes made up his muzzle. This gave him a rather phallic shape that Clive and Elsa had snickered about in the early days, but when one after another of Fred's predecessors were stillborn, the couple started to find this suggestive appearance less and less funny.

Fred's manatee-like snout jiggled as he snuffled the air, and he emitted a muffled chortling noise a little like a dolphin. His creators had long since agreed that when discussing the recombinant DNA cocktail that produced Fred's family, they would be as unspecific as the situation allowed. They had a reasonable claim to confidentiality, as does anyone working on a patent, but they also sensed that the more Fred and Ginger were identified with existing animals, the more Clive and Elsa would have to contend with human prejudice. To some, a cow is sacred; to others, it's dinner. The rat is a treasured pet, or a plague-carrier. Many people recoil from reptiles, and who would want to swallow a pill that was even a tiny part cockroach protein? Sentimentality is the enemy of science. The two scientists already got enough grief from the pearl-clutchers who thought of DNA as God's private property. They didn't need anyone hassling them about whether Fred and Ginger were kosher, for instance, before they even entered the marketing phase.

Clive lowered Fred into the tank and watched as the little fellow got his bearings. The proud parent hoisted a victorious thumbs-up toward the observation window with a grin:

"We're good!"

On the other side of the pane, Clive's little brother Gavin grinned proudly—his "mini me", as Elsa called him behind his back. Not that the tall, lanky young man was especially mini, but he took after Clive so slavishly as to be like a low-res facsimile. Clive found Elsa's observation a little annoying, and unnecessary; Gavin was a good guy, supportive, hardworking, and most importantly, never jealous. He was completely satisfied to be part of Clive's success, whether he shared the spotlight or not. Frankly, Clive thought Elsa might be the jealous one, as an only child who knew no sorority. He could forgive her for being a little lonely, even if a lone wolf like herself would never admit to it. And she shouldn't have to, as long as she had Clive to keep her company.

"Ginger, meet Fred. Fred, meet Ginger," Elsa said as she zoomed in on the rear of the tank. With a soft gurgling sound, Ginger snuck shyly out of the plastic shelter and into view. Ginger was larger than Fred—naturally, since she was older, but the scene reminded Elsa of how human girls matured faster than boys. She felt an odd pang of sympathy, recalling the autumn when she returned to school to find that she and the other young ladies had attained a certain size and shape, while their male classmates looked like little gnomes in comparison. She laughed off the awkward memory, refocusing on the meet-cute happening on her video monitor.

Fred crept toward Ginger as she emerged fully into the light. She acknowledged her guest by rearing up, displaying several sets of subtly protruding mammary glands. Then, she began to undulate—a disturbingly sensual movement that squeezed something up from within her. To the astonishment of her rapt audience, a small opening appeared in her lobed face, admitting a slick, slender extremity that unfurled like a fern. The wide, flat pad at the end, with its intricately rippling border, reminded Elsa of Ernst Haeckel's elegant 19th century illustrations of deep-sea creatures. Fred and Ginger were works of art.

An emboldened Fred inched toward his date. He produced his own translucent pink tendril and reached out for Ginger. Clive stiffened. "What are they doing?" he whispered.

"Imprinting," Elsa replied without taking her eyes off the new couple.

Though they both thought of Fred and Ginger as products rather than pets, Elsa had some education in animal behavior. What she didn't already know from her farmland upbringing, she had supplemented in preparation for this very moment. She never left anything to chance.

"See? Love at first sight."

Clive watched in awe as Fred and Ginger's feelers formed a strange embrace, barely touching, as if they held between them an invisible orb. They twittered peacefully. Elsa's mouth formed a particular smile that Clive knew well. It expressed the unique pleasure of being right.

The elevator doors opened to the executive suite of the towering Newstead Pharmaceuticals building. Clive and Elsa stepped into the reception area, the scent of orchids tickling their noses as their boots sank into a plush carpet that created a sacred silence. They briefly imagined this atmosphere of power and luxury infusing a future office of their own—before the spell was broken by William Barlow tumbling out of the elevator behind them.

"I really wish you guys would fill me in. I like to think we're a team. I like to think I'm a sounding board!"

"But you're so much more than that, Barlow!" Elsa snickered.

Clive and Elsa didn't turn around as their senior project manager stammered and staggered behind them. They didn't so much dislike him as they loved teasing him. Barlow kept their lab's daily operations running smoothly, giving them the space to think and create, but his terminal anal-retentiveness and kicked-puppy disposition made the urge to bully him irresistible. They also enjoyed the way his squaresville appearance offset their punk glamour, which they felt separated them from the rest of the geek squad. Barlow's chronically furrowed brow creased even deeper at the sight of the couple's outfits, on this day of all days:

Clive wore a gray tartan blazer in a shameless impression of Malcolm McLaren, over a black tee shirt with white text in imitation of the PMRC's iconic Parental Warning sticker. It read "BRING **NOTHING** TO THE TABLE", referencing some obscure indie movie that Barlow knew from experience not to ask about, and that he thought sent exactly the wrong message for today's meeting. The lank, black forelocks that Clive purposefully arranged around his languid eyes wouldn't do him any favors, either. Elsa's look was more formal, but in exactly the wrong way: A sharp black leather sport coat over a black silk blouse with a bold, blood-red necktie gave her a fascistic flair that could add the wrong tone to a conversation about genetic engineering. Her long, blonde hair was pushed back behind a pair of birch-framed aviator sunglasses propped above her porcelain brow; possibly, she held her nose so high just to keep them from sliding down her face.

"Relax," Clive said, with a practiced nonchalance. "This is just another dog-and-pony show."

"We could splice a dog and a pony!" Elsa giggled.

"It could take our meetings!"

"Maybe I can help you with your publicity."

Barlow wedged himself between them, waving the latest issue of Wired Magazine in their faces accusatively. Its cover featured Clive and Elsa posing in sleek sci-fi catsuits, gazing boldly into the future. The headline read "EPIC NERDS: THE FUTURE OF GENETICS". Barlow paged over to their interview and huffed in dismay.

"'If God didn't want us to explore his domain, why'd he give us the map?'"

The couple snatched up the magazine eagerly.

"Bumper sticker wisdom," Elsa chuckled.

"I get it, and I am totally with you guys on every level. But

Joan Charot can make or break our project without even blinking!"

Barlow attempted meaningful eye contact, but Clive and Elsa were too absorbed in their own high gloss reflections to notice. He wiped his glistening brow with the back of his hand and wondered how they could be so unbothered. This was a big day. *The* big day. An hour from now, they could double their research & development budget, or they could be out in the proverbial street. He knew the Wired hype wasn't for nothing; they *were* on track for a major breakthrough, and everything *seemed* to be going their way. But Barlow didn't have as much confidence that the sun would rise tomorrow as these two seemed to have in their own inevitable victory.

"We should all be a little nervous, as in *survival instinct* nervous. So come on, what are you guys up to?"

"I don't wanna spoil the surprise," Clive replied wryly. "C'mon, Bar!"

"You love surprises, don't you?" Elsa cooed, slipping her arm around Barlow's shoulders even though he was a little damp.

"No. Surprises make me nauseous."

Clive and Elsa struggled to keep their cool as their presentation played on the laptop of the feared and revered Joan Charot, Newstead's Chief Operating Officer. It was a promotional masterpiece: slick, graphic, and futuristic. As the silhouettes of various flora and fauna danced with double helices on Joan's screen, Elsa took a deep breath, then began the call-and-response pitch that she and Clive had rehearsed. He had to smile; this wasn't Elsa's naturally dry conversational voice. It was her *marketing voice*, brighter, friendlier, more feminine. More seductive to those with deep pockets.

"Over the course of the last three years, our lab has combined the DNA from a variety of species to create a completely new life form."

Clive took his cue. "And as you know, Ginger has exceeded

all expectations in her ability to produce medicinal proteins for livestock."

A 3D model of their chimera appeared, juxtaposed with protein strands that morphed into colorful capsules—strands of CD356, to be exact — the substance that had shown so much promise for the treatment of various cattle ailments.

"What you *don't* know is," Elsa rejoined, "since the birth of Fred, we have an upgraded splicing technique that can be applied to the most sophisticated of organisms. Namely..."

Leonardo da Vinci's "Vitruvian Man" filled Joan's screen.

"...human beings."

"Whoa, whoa, whoa!" Barlow nearly jumped out of his frumpy suit. "Let's not get too far ahead of ourselves."

Clive held the line, oozing his trademark chill. "By incorporating human DNA into the hybrid template, we can begin to address any number of genetically influenced diseases."

"Parkinson's, Alzheimer's, diabetes...even some forms of cancer," Elsa added, daring Barlow to dismiss such utopian possibilities.

Joan Charot leaned back in her chair; her face eclipsed by the velvet shadows of her boardroom. Her silhouette nearly vanished into a large painting of twisting black tree branches against a canvas of gray silk. The space, with its strategically placed lights gleaming off the varnish of the round table that dwarfed their party of three, was engineered specifically to add weight to an audience with the powerful COO. She sighed softly. The sound seemed to bring the whole world to a standstill. Clive, Elsa, and Barlow turned toward her. They neither blinked nor breathed. An eternal present stretched out between them. Joan's placid features betrayed nothing of her thoughts. There was no translating the meaning of her executive silence; it was like being in the presence of the Sphinx. Whatever happened next would either seal their fate or secure their future.

"Well," she said, fixing her eyes on Clive, then on Elsa. Her

French accent lent her extra gravity with her Anglo audience, and she knew it. She could have been twice their age for all they knew, as she was timelessly beautiful, and the years had taught her the power of suspense. Finally, Joan purred, "I can't tell you how…excited we are."

Clive made a herculean effort not to react as his comrade leaned forward hungrily.

"The entire board is thrilled with the progress you've made, which is why we are so anxious to move on to Phase 2."

Elsa blinked. "Phase 2?"

"The product stage. We need to isolate the gene in Ginger and Fred that produces your magic protein. We are shutting down the splicing facilities and retooling your labs for intensive chemical analysis."

Barlow relaxed audibly, triggering a homicidal urge in Elsa.

"*Shutting down?*" Clive repeated blankly.

"I don't understand," Elsa bit off. "We're handing you the medical breakthrough of the century! We could begin to—"

"Elsa," Barlow interjected in his most infuriatingly rational tone, "we all know that can't happen right now. The moral outrage would be completely out of control! I mean, regulators and politicians would tear us to pieces."

Elsa shot him a look that burned off his patronizing smile before turning to Joan. "Please. If we don't use human DNA now, someone else will."

"*La passion,*" Joan sighed with weary amusement, and rose to her feet. "*C'est ça la jeunesse, eh?* Look, we'd love to go there— to shoot for incredible medical breakthroughs. Of course we would!" She pointed an impeccably manicured nail at the space between them, as if to conjure a vision of the future. "You put a viable livestock product on the shelves, and then we will talk about a twenty-year plan to save the world."

Elsa's cheeks glowed with anger as Joan crossed behind her and Clive. The COO placed her hands firmly on their shoulders as she concluded, "Right now, we need to start Phase 2...and you are the only ones who can do it."

There was nothing more to say.

Elsa would have blown open the elevator doors with pure rage were they a second slower to open. She was much shorter than Clive, but he could barely keep up with her as she stormed toward the parking lot. He was just as frustrated as she was, but with her, things could get a little scary.

"We could quit. Go to Hamilton-Splinter," he offered.

"Newstead owns our patents. We'd lose everything."

Clive caught her by the elbow and spun her toward him. "Well? What?"

He ducked slightly to look into her eyes with his best "be reasonable" expression—a negotiating technique that had never, ever worked on her. He should have known better than to think his defeated shrug would soften her indignation. Elsa locked him in a determined stare that he knew all too well.

"I am not spending the next five years digging through pig shit for enteric proteins."

Clive held her gaze. He couldn't guess exactly what she was thinking, or if she had even formed a plan yet. All he knew for sure, at that moment, were two things:

First, that when Elsa got that look in her eye, nothing could stop her from getting what she wanted.

And second, that wherever that look led them, trouble followed.

But, more often than not, it was *good* trouble. He inhaled deeply and took in the lovely face of the woman he'd been waking up with since their undergrad years; someone who never let him quit, no matter the odds. A woman whose sheer force of will had brought them right up to the brink of nothing less than a medical revolution. The face of the person he had chosen to live beside and, he hoped, to die beside. He exhaled.

"Neither am I."

2

The ostentatious steel-and-neon sign outside the Nucleic Exchange Research + Development Laboratory was more impressive than the building itself: a squat, sterile block of white that in no way suggested the birthplace of humanity's future. In the lot, at that dusky hour, the only sign of life was the couple's 1976 AMC Gremlin in "Big Bad Orange"—something Clive loved almost as much as he loved Elsa (so she spared his feelings by ignoring its notoriously poor handling). Deep in the bowels of the lab, lit only by the cold glow of computer monitors, the couple plunged into their forbidden experiment.

Clive wheeled his office chair manically from one screen to another, slurping cold coffee and chomping on an even colder slice of pizza. He had to raise his voice to be heard over the crunching, clanging electronic music that he claimed helped him think: a mathy collision of vintage synthesizers, oddball analog instruments, and brutalized household objects that sounded like pure noise to his colleagues, but that he insisted was music to his ears.

"What's the profile?"

"Jane Doe," Elsa replied as she labeled a test tube HUMAN

FEMALE c.2069. "Anonymous female donor. Clean medical and heredity. The usual."

"Dime a dozen."

"One in a million."

They locked eyes as she handed him the tube. He inserted it into a centrifuge rack, and they held their breath as he lowered the rack into a circulating bath. The plastic tray spun on the water's surface like a merry-go-round, bobbing gently above the heating coil that brought the specimen quickly and safely up to incubation temperature. All they had to do now was wait.

⊗ Human / Animal Hybrid Splice 35645_f
UNSUCCESSFUL

Clive threw up his hands and sighed bitterly at this now-familiar conclusion. He rubbed his eyes, which ached from the endlessly scrolling code and flashy graphics. The high-definition microscopy feed seemed like a good idea when they shelled out for it—investors loved to see anything that smacked of science fiction—but now it produced only bad news. The monitors showed animal base pairs being sadly rejected, over and over again, by the human sample; the DNA strands split as expected, but the splice wasn't happening. It was like a 24-hour broadcast of the world's worst prom.

Clive was having trouble fending off despair. Dehydration was setting in, too, from the salty leftovers and stagnant urn coffee, and his skin felt cold and tight. He shoveled chilly wads of old lo mein into his mouth, hoping to suppress his system's desperate demands for actual nutrition. Grease clung to his mouth. He needed a change of clothes and a shower, and the computer's grating failure chime wasn't doing his growing headache any favors.

"It's not working."

"What enzyme are you using?"

"It's not the cleavage, they're digesting fine."

"So?" Elsa's energy level remained mysteriously unchanged. It was a quality Clive found equally admirable and annoying. She was simply immune to doubt.

"The human Alu sequences don't want to bond with foreigners."

"So what? We'll use a ligase other than T4. We'll *make* them."

"Oh, we'll just *'make them'*," Clive repeated dejectedly.

"Yeah, we will. You know why? Because Wired doesn't interview losers."

Elsa wrapped her arms around his neck and smiled encouragingly, sharing her unflagging willpower by osmosis. The warmth of her body rejuvenated him somewhat, though it also made him long for bed.

"Sometimes I forget those basic scientific principles," he chuckled. He marveled at the second wind she could bring out of him. He wouldn't give up; he couldn't. She'd never let him.

⊗ Human / Animal Hybrid Splice 07263_a
UNSUCCESSFUL

"UGH!"

The unbroken chain of disappointments was finally wearing away Elsa's preternatural confidence. She spun around helplessly, holding her throbbing head. How long had they been at it? What day was it, even?

Watching his eternally optimistic companion losing altitude woke Clive up. She couldn't carry him all the time; it was his turn to pick up the slack. He stormed over to the sound system and killed the mind-numbing electronic beats. The ensuing silence was deafening.

"This retarded, fascist *übermusik* is the fucking problem," he spat haughtily. "Got us thinking in circles." He popped open his tape deck and slammed in a new cassette.

The lilting sound of an alto saxophone got Elsa's attention, though she was more inspired by Clive's renewed vigor than she was by jazz. At least this was easy to listen to. She didn't care as much for music as did her partner, and frankly, she wasn't always sure if he enjoyed everything that he said he did, or if he was just being fashionably unfashionable. His choice of tunes could be like his whining, hissing, frankly antique tape deck, or the toxic orange monstrosity in the lot outside; it wasn't easy to know if he was being performatively ironic, or if he really had some esoteric reason for loving his outsidery collectibles. Privately, Elsa thought that maybe she herself was one of his culty fetish objects: a challenging, difficult little thing, obscure and hard to work with…but somehow, he saw something in her that made him happy. Something that perhaps only he understood. Mysterious as it was, she didn't take it for granted.

Rifling through a filing cabinet, Elsa found a fix for her waning blood sugar. A day-glo box of tiny, rainbow-hued candies—little more than coagulated nodules of sugar and citric acid, though they were anthropomorphized on the package as bipedal, hippo-like creatures. Clive found it extremely funny that this was his sophisticated girlfriend's favorite food, but his amusement didn't dampen her cravings. Shaking out a handful of the tiny treats, she rejoined the fight.

"You're right. We have been dancing to the wrong beat! Try this—"

Clive spun around to see Elsa holding a fresh ligase sample.

"—M3."

Her electric smile filled him with hope. Nothing could stop them now.

Clive had almost nodded off, head in hand, when he heard Elsa yawn. His eyes fluttered open, but he was completely out of gas. Neither coffee, nor candy, nor his partner's boundless ambition could save him from the existential ennui that had swallowed him up. This was the end.

"It's not working," he groaned. His eyes wouldn't focus, and he was using up his remaining life force imagining ways to convince Elsa that it was time to go home.

The computer chimed softly.

☑ Human / Animal Hybrid Splice 010448_p SUCCESSFUL

Reality seemed to warp around Clive as adrenaline shot through his system. He felt like he was being sucked into a reverse zoom in a Twilight Zone episode. Could this be real? Had he fallen asleep and dreamed it?

"Wait a second…*it's happening.*"

Elsa was at his side in a flash. "Why now?"

"I don't know, but they're on fire! We got the right temperature, and that enzyme—"

"They're changing partners!"

The couple watched the feed in awe.

"Everyone dances with everyone."

"You are Bob fucking Fosse!"

Elsa flung herself into Clive's lap and he held her tight, promising himself he would never doubt her again. The future was wide open.

Clive opened the door to the refrigerated storage room, allowing Elsa to wheel in the waist-high Dewar canister containing their greatest achievement to date, which slumbered safely in liquid nitrogen. He could hardly believe that this everyday object held the key to their future. To *everyone's* future, in fact. They'd show Barlow, and they'd show Joan Charot, too: Those cowards would be crushed to realize that they'd settled for livestock medicine, when Clive and Elsa were literally a day away from a potential cure for cancer. There would be no "moral outrage" about human gene splicing when the world learned how many lives the couple's daring would save. No more handwringing about meddling in God's domain. They'd go from outlaws to heroes overnight…if only they could find a way to unveil their discovery without getting arrested.

"Biotechnology's most startling breakthrough in decades… on ice."

Clive noticed an unusual catch in Elsa's voice. They'd achieved their dream—the first step of it, anyway—and yet catharsis still seemed out of reach. It was bittersweet to have to hide their incredible discovery from a world that so badly needed it, but also…did they really know what they were doing? Elsa seemed to sense Clive scrutinizing her expression, and she bowed her head. She must have shared his turmoil. But they had to be right…*right?*

The only people who really worried about genetic engineering were pretentious hippies and religious bumpkins who thought that if God wanted us to fly, then we'd have been born with wings. And all that precious concern about eugenics was just reactionary paranoia, wasn't it? If you asked someone with Hodgkin's lymphoma whether they were more worried about seeing their children grow up, or about a hypothetical future full of blue-eyed babies… It was ridiculous to even consider the argument.

Other, darker thoughts fought for Clive's attention. On an ordinary day, he could shake them off, but this was no such day. Deep down, he was too smart to believe that the worries about their work were just paranoid *Boys From Brazil* fantasies. Taken to its logical conclusion, the ability to curate human genetics could have the consequence of eradicating not only destructive diseases, but whole types of human beings. The trouble came from the debate over what was a disease, versus what was simply a difference. People with achondroplasia did not see themselves as tragic freaks and objected fiercely to being pathologized as such. They posed a valid question: Why was it so much easier for people to imagine a world without little people than it was to ask for more ADA-compliant cities?

Activism was also on the rise among intersex individuals

who protested the horrors of "corrective" surgeries forced on them at birth by a healthcare system that saw them as unwanted anomalies. An unwitting victim of these procedures could suffer lifelong dysphoria without ever knowing why, or who, they could have been. They should be acknowledged as normal and natural, not to be carved out of existence through genital mutilation *or* genetic engineering. And not only morphological, but neurological differences could also land one on the proverbial chopping block: Recently, MIT researchers had isolated a gene in macaque monkeys that they connected with autism. For all the challenges they faced in a neurotypical world, autistic people didn't see themselves as the problem. Neurodivergent activists had their hands full with controversial groups like Autism Speaks, which framed their distinctive wiring as a disorder to be destroyed through disturbing methods akin to conversion therapy. They would not be pleased to hear that people like themselves could be edited out of the human spectrum before they were even born.

The latter point hit close to home for Clive and his brother, Gavin. They had often discussed the possibility that they were autistic. They had never been tested, being "high functioning" overachievers who caused their family no concern, but they believed neurodivergence could be a part of what made them stand out. It may have given them the advantage of sustained, almost monomaniacal focus throughout their grueling academic careers; it may have been the reason that they could come up with unconventional questions and answers that their class-mates failed to find in their neurotypical ruts. Clive entertained the notion that Elsa shared their condition, although she wasn't interested in talking about it.

In addition to her propensity for hyperfocusing on esoteric subjects, she also had the flat affect that was part of the autism cliché, and a bluntness that bordered on rude. Personally, Clive found it all pretty sexy, and he loved the way she confounded people who expected someone so pretty and petite to be sweet and submissive. She seemed to enjoy her ability to surprise people in this way, but he knew it wasn't for show. She simply didn't relate to other people like he could, and he often found himself smoothing ruffled feathers to protect her from fights she didn't even mean to pick. She may also have had a more stereotypically challenging childhood, as someone obviously different from Clive. She didn't seem to have had the same kinds of supportive, almost sycophantic parents who sent Gavin and himself skyrocketing through elite science programs. He suspected as much from the fact that Elsa had never spoken about her parents at all.

Clive and Elsa hadn't come this far just to help enforce universal standards of normality. Even if their work *could be* extrapolated into ways of purging achondroplasia and autism from the human profile, that wasn't their problem. There were plenty of regulatory bodies and human rights orgs in place to deal with all that. Clive and Elsa's purpose was to eliminate meaningless suffering and loss of life. And besides, this wasn't 1939; they lived in the future now. The eugenics question was a separate issue altogether from the project of saving the world from needless misery. Surely, even the most fearful Luddite could see their point of view.

But, of course, there would be no debate to have at all if Clive and Elsa were both in prison.

Clive looked down at Elsa's delicate hands. She was white knuckling the Dewar canister's handles and gnawing at her lower lip.

"Well," He sighed with a resigned smile. "At least now we know we can do it. Right?"

So maybe they couldn't show the world what they'd accomplished just yet. And they couldn't save any lives with it right this minute. Maybe not for a while, not until they'd found a way to legitimize it for the Luddites. But they finally had proof of concept. They knew what to do, and how to do it again. That was more than enough for now. *Right, Elsa?*

Elsa's trembling eased, then disappeared altogether. Satisfaction settled over her features...and warped her mouth into a crooked grin. Still gripping the canister's handles, she began to back away from him.

"Elsa..."

The look in her eye sent a chill down Clive's spine. A mischievous twinkle that he usually found adorable, but definitely not at that moment. She turned slowly—and sprang back down the corridor away from him, shoving the canister ahead of her.

"Elsa, come on. What are you doing?"

Trying not to panic, Clive power-walked after her as she careened toward...*oh God, what is she thinking? Stay calm, don't spook her. She'll listen to reason. She has to.*

"Come on, I don't have the energy to play with you right now, OK?"

Clive's heart leapt into his throat when he heard the electronic beeping of a keypad. He broke into a run, but too late, as the door to the birthing chamber closed in his face. He frantically keyed in the code, and—nothing.

"Did you recode the locks?"

"I recoded the locks!" came her chipper reply.

Elsa was already extracting their freshly spliced sample from the canister while Clive pounded helplessly on the door. Freezing mist poured over her gloves as she grasped it with her tongs and swiftly transported it to the servo-guided injection needle that had previously fathered Fred and Ginger. She'd have had an easier time if Clive were there; the thick plastic casing for the needle and its control panel sat at about Elsa's eye level atop a wheeled stand, but she nimbly slid the sample into place. Then she dollied the needle over to the artificial womb— the Biomechanical Extroutero Thermal Incubator, or BETI for short: a heavy, oblong tank holding about 50 gallons of amniotic fluid, where Fred and Ginger once gestated.

It hung from a sturdy metal armature in the center of the

room, sporting yards of tubes and wires, and was flanked by three video screens: an EKG readout and microscopy feed on one side, and on the other, a vital signs monitor. Floating near the top of the illuminated tank was BETI's artificial uterus, a dark, wrinkled sac like a sinking dirigible, sandwiched between observation windows. One pane was decorated with a vinyl sticker featuring a Bettie Page lookalike, smiling not very maternally up at the voyeuristic clinician.

"Elsa, seriously! This is what's known in couples' therapy as *emotional hijacking*. Elsa?" Clive struggled to sound rational, persuasive, in control—but it wasn't really "emotional hijacking". It was actual hijacking. Grand larceny. The end of the world!

OVUM READY FOR INSERTION declared the needle's LED readout with an encouraging chime as the servo needle docked.

"Come on, this is illegal. We're gonna go to jail for this. Open the door!" Clive nearly fell on his face when the door suddenly swung open. Elsa grinned.

"*Human cloning* is illegal! *This* won't be human. Not entirely."

"What are you doing?" Clive was horrified to see BETI and the needle already in flagrante delicto.

"Relax, we won't take it to term! We just need to know if we can generate a sustainable embryo. Then we destroy it. No one will ever know."

Somehow, he didn't find this very convincing. "Then what's the point? What's the point if you can't publish?"

"To be sure we really did it! To know for sure."

Clive stared into BETI's tank. A bad feeling was forming in the pit of his stomach. A doomed presentiment whose cold tentacles slithered through his entrails. It wasn't what he thought he would feel when this moment finally came.

"You're telling me you don't need to know?"

He floundered. "It's not so simple...there are moral considerations!"

Elsa's solicitous pandering transformed into open defiance. She stared up at Clive. "Millions of people are suffering and dying with no hope. We might be sitting on the key to saving them. What are the moral considerations of that?"

The injection needle began to click off a countdown. If no action were taken within 30 seconds, the operation would self-abort. BETI'S microscopy feed showed the ovum waiting inside for its injection, an innocent little blob filled with untold potential. A possible end to very real, very present global pain—or a Pandora's box of ethical perils that, for now, were speculative at best. Clive's hands hovered over the needle's keypad as the timer ticked down. Could he really afford to stand in the way of progress, in the name of problems that were themselves unborn? Alternatively, could he stand to look back on this day and remember that he had taken no part in it?

With one second to go, Clive hit the ENTER key. BETI's monitor displayed the magnified needle punching through the wall of the ovum and retracting just as violently.

OVUM INSEMINATED

Clive was at a loss for words, except one.
"Fuck."
"Exactly," Elsa replied breathlessly.

>B.E.T.I. INJECTION SEQUENCE
>BLASTOCYST IMPLANTATION

The new parents had no time to reflect before BETI's monitor announced the next phase of the process. They watched a crudely animated diagram of the fertilized egg being slowly transported to its new home in the waiting uterus. It was oddly anticlimactic; the stark geometric shapes on the screen could not approximate the life-changing event taking place within the machine. Still, Elsa's eyes glowed triumphantly. All was said and done. Nothing could possibly go wrong.

"How's it coming, little brother?"

"Good." Gavin barely stirred from his post at the incubator.

"How's Fred doing?"

"Our boy is growing into a fine young man!" he quipped.

Clive peered through the incubator's clear plastic hood at his artificial son, who had grown beefier recently, more tumescent. The innocent little critter had no idea that he was only feet away from a graveyard containing his fallen fellows: a closet where an eclectic collection of glass jars and bottles held the remains of abortive projects in various states of gestation. Some might be mistaken for fruit preserves; others had formed masses of tangled tentacles, grasping avian claws, and gasping frog-like maws; still others were little more than a handful of imperceptible cells floating in formalin. More than a few of the containers were emptied champagne bottles from premature celebrations. Handwritten labels bore the names of famous couples: *Sid & Nancy, Bogey and Bacall, Adam + Eve,* and so on.

"And Phase 2?"

"Don't worry," Gavin replied reassuringly. "We'll nail that gene."

"Good, man. Double helix!"

The brothers slapped hands in a spiraling motion, the secret handshake they performed with even more pleasure when Elsa wasn't around to laugh at them. As Clive turned to walk away, Gavin called him back.

"Hey, uh...I can't help but wonder what you and Elsa have been so busy with."

He tacked on a respectful smile. He was always careful not to come between the couple, but something felt off lately. Clive seemed agitated, though not exactly excited. Gavin studied his expression. Some strange secret danced behind his tired eyes.

"We're building you your very own special friend, Gavin," Clive answered with a cryptic grin.

"Thank you." Gavin nodded emphatically. "I have been *so lonely*."

"Not for long!" Clive said as he turned to walk away.

Weird, Gavin thought. Considering their line of work…was that really a joke? Gavin imagined waking up in his cramped bachelor pad and being followed to the kitchen by a retriever-sized tardigrade begging for breakfast as he brewed a pot of coffee. Trying to teach it that it wasn't allowed on the furniture, and that his beloved paratrooper boots were not chew toys. *At least they don't shed*, he thought. But still…should he ask his brother what he meant?

Clive had already vanished.

In the dim, green light of the birthing chamber, Elsa circled BETI with her clipboard, staring at the artificial uterus. The EKG monitor beeped out a rhythm for her endless march around the machine, piercing the low, constant hum. She squinted at the vitals readout, nervously jotting down the slightest fluctuation. BETI's video feed showed something that looked like a little phosphorescent croissant, flexing now and then in its protective amnion.

This must be what it's like for expectant mothers, Elsa mused. *Worried. Obsessed. Kind of…in love.*

Elsa had never shown the slightest interest in normal procreation. Actually, it was a good thing that Clive was so attracted to her, because sex could be sort of an ordeal. Where most people prefer a little spontaneity, Clive had learned to sit tight each time while Elsa visited the bathroom to insert a diaphragm, spermicide, and sponge, and to pick up a condom for him. Many ambitious young women are nervous about unplanned pregnancy, but Elsa was positively phobic. She defended her routine by saying that she wouldn't let anything take her away from this early phase of her career, not a pregnancy, not an abortion, nothing.

Once or twice Clive broached the subject of tubal ligation, but her answer was still negative—even though they both knew it was a relatively easy procedure that could have her home the same day. She cited obscure statistics on post-op conception, the increased likelihood of it for someone young and healthy like herself, and the potential for suffering an ectopic pregnancy. He knew that these were all slim possibilities, but he always relented anyway, letting Elsa do whatever made her feel comfortable being with him. He trusted that there were reasons for her idiosyncrasies, which she would share if and when she was ready.

For her part, Elsa was grateful that Clive knew better than to interrogate her about anything she didn't volunteer first. He was patient and gentle, and he respected her privacy. Still, he wasn't an idiot, and from certain offhanded innuendos, he seemed to have guessed that maternity had not agreed with her mother. Well, better for him to guess than for Elsa to have to describe it to him.

Her reverie was suddenly shattered by the piercing cry of the flatlining EKG. The fetus had come to an unnatural rest. Fear struck Elsa so hard she saw stars.

"Come on, come on, come on, come on."

The EKG whined urgently. Its flat scan streamed across the screen, and the little crescent remained deathly still. The sounds of the machines were almost drowned out by the sound of Elsa's own terrified heartbeat, which some distant, dissociated part of her noticed with amazement.

It's so loud! How can that be? Why don't I hear it all the time? Could Clive hear it if he were here now? Have I ever heard it like this? No... Wait. Yes. Holy shit. I haven't been so afraid since...since...

Then, just as suddenly, everything returned to normal. The EKG regained its natural rhythm—the readings seemed even stronger, healthier somehow—and the glowing fetus on the monitor pulsed with renewed vitality. It looked to Elsa like a little beating heart.

Outside their apartment, the snow fell thick and deep. It was early evening, but the heavy precipitation occluded the waning winter sunlight and sucked up every sound. All Elsa could hear was the incessant rapping of Clive's knuckles against his filing cabinet. He slumped on their couch in a trance, captivated by the experimental tunes piping through his expensive cans. He had tried to explain the difference between technical metal and mathcore, and mathcore and math rock, and progressive rock and progressive jazz to Elsa a few times, but the only thing she really needed to know was that she didn't want to listen to any of them. He obediently limited these subgenres to headphones, but that didn't prevent him from externalizing his appreciation for them. He banged out a mindless rhythm on the filing cabinet, atop which a gaggle of designer toys rattled against one another and fell to the floor under the seismic force of Clive's enthusiasm.

"Hey, can you not do that?" Elsa called in a measured tone. *Bang, bang, bang.* "Can you not do that?" *BANG, BANG, BANG.* She shook out a handful of her favorite psychedelic hippo snacks, and the motion caught his attention.

"Huh?" he grunted, forgetting to remove his headphones.

"Don't do that."

He uncovered one ear. "What?"

"*Don't do that.*"

"It's my Zeppelin Interpolation! Come on, you don't like it?" he asked innocently, knowing Elsa wouldn't remember the band name.

"Zeppelin crashed and burned before I was born," she smirked, ever the proud philistine.

Clive's friends sometimes insinuated that Elsa might be a little hard to live with, and he always thought to himself, *They have no idea what she puts up with.* He scooped up his fallen soldiers—arty collectibles from sculptor Yukinori Dehara and toymaker Tokidoki (an Italian designer doing an anime pastiche, as Clive loved to tell people)—and returned to Planet Earth. Elsa settled next to him on the couch and placed her laptop on the coffee table before them.

"Check this out. It's near the distillery." She was browsing for lofts again and showed him one that offered the space they needed and the slick, minimalist flavor that they enjoyed. "I fucking love it!"

"Yeah, it's cool."

"You don't sound that enthusiastic."

"I don't know," he shrugged, looking around at the installation he had painstakingly created out of plastic sculptures and screen prints from young graffiti artists transitioning from the streets to the gallery scene. Clive had always had more of a nesting instinct than Elsa. "I just don't wanna move again anytime soon."

"We've been here for seven years!"

He squinted skeptically at her screen. "That place just doesn't seem big enough."

"It's twice the size of our apartment. More than enough room for all our stuff."

"But, you know, for…down the road," Clive said, gesturing abstractly.

Elsa sighed. She might have known their new endeavor would bring up certain issues, no matter how settled they seemed before. She looked him frankly in the eye.

"You're talking about a kid, aren't you?"

Clive shrugged blithely, as if he didn't know perfectly well what she would say. "Is that so unreasonable?"

"Yeah, it is. Because I'm the one who has to have it." Elsa hated to repeat herself, but she still felt a pang of remorse at the sight of Clive sulking. "Look, I love this place. But I don't want to bend my life to suit some third party that doesn't even exist yet!"

Clive didn't argue. Not with words, anyway. He stared into her eyes tenderly. "Come on. Come here."

She let him pull her into his lap and stroke her face. The falling snow had an insulating effect; the prickly topic could not pierce the cozy, Christmasy atmosphere between them. He pushed her falling locks behind her ears and felt her relax as he crushed her against his chest. Elsa didn't like to be touched by anyone but Clive. It was an honor he took very seriously, although they still joked about getting her a hug machine. Animal behaviorist Temple Grandin had made revolutionary innovations in livestock management using her ability to hyper-empathize with animals. Her system involved "squeeze chutes": adjustable cages whose firm pressure reduced stress in cattle. Grandin understood the soothing effect of being held, but her classically autistic sensory processing disorder made human contact unbearable. How could someone like her enjoy the benefits of a hug without the mortifying ordeal of *being* hugged? Her answer: the hug machine, a contraption made from cushioned boards and straps that could pleasantly squash and subdue an overstimulated person. In the absence of such a device, Elsa had Clive.

"What's the worst that could happen?" He was laying it on thick as he felt her melt against him. A coy smile crept across her face.

"How about after we crack male pregnancy?"

Clive laughed in spite of himself. "And ruin this perfect figure?"

"You're a hypocrite," Elsa giggled.

"No, *you're* a hypocrite!"

They kissed, and Clive felt himself swoon. How long had it

been since they'd had sex? They'd spent so much time at the lab lately, it felt like they rarely even took off their shoes. Too much left-brain activity kept their emotions on ice, suppressing their senses and instincts. The feeling of Elsa's weight against his body made Clive painfully aware of how touch-starved he'd become. They began to fall into a familiar rhythm—when Clive's cell phone chimed.

"Who is it?" Elsa murmured as he glanced at the screen. "Ignore it."

She felt him freeze beneath her.

"What?"

"…it's BETI."

3

Clive and Elsa were glad they still had their galoshes on when they slid into the birthing chamber to find BETI hemorrhaging amniotic fluid in a heavy rain from the overhanging irrigation tubes. The bleating emergency klaxon and the eye-watering, chlorine-like smell in the air overloaded their senses.

"Holy shit! What's going on?" Clive gasped, tossing Elsa her scrubs.

"It's coming out," she grunted, pulling on gloves.

BETI's monitor streamed an urgent, repeated message:

>>PREPARING FOR AMNIOTOMY
>>PREPARING FOR AMNIOTOMY
>>PREPARING FOR AMNIOTOMY
>>PREPARING FOR AMNIOTOMY
>>PREPARING FOR AMNIOTOMY

"What? It can't do that. It's not due for months!" Clive blustered.

"Well, tell that to the fetus." Elsa's eyes widened at the sight of the video feed underneath the spiking EKG monitor. "Oh god, it's huge!"

They didn't need the monitor to tell them that. Something very large and powerful was struggling to break free of the uterus and threatening to rip it out of the sockets that held it in place.

"I thought you were keeping tabs!"

"I was! It wasn't that big this morning."

BETI's occupant was straining its capacity, dangerously stretching the uterus and displacing fluid at an alarming rate.

"There's too much pressure," Clive shouted over the screaming machinery. "It'll kill it!"

Elsa's characteristic decisiveness abandoned her. Blinking lights and clashing alarms jarred her thinking as her head swam with emergency measures, any of which could spell catastrophe. An irrigation hose broke free and drenched her in warm, acrid-smelling liquid. The physical shock refocused her.

"OK, we're gonna have to do this manually."

Clive wrestled with the valves on BETI's undercarriage. "It's not depressurizing!"

"Alright."

Elsa approached BETI's rubberized delivery aperture and penetrated it, pushing in her arm up to the elbow. An unexpected flood of sense memories assailed her as she flashed back to inseminating dairy cows on the family farm: Her body more than her brain recalled reaching into a heifer's rectum and internally palpating the vulva open to create a clear path for the catheter. It was a daunting task, as an unwary cattleman could come away with a broken arm. But, while Elsa had no fondness for farm life, she always relished the chance to show off her courage and iron stomach. Then, as now, there was no way to watch what she was doing, but the critical difference today was that she had no way of knowing what she might find inside.

"Can you feel it?"

"I can't…it's slippery. It's—*AH!*"

Elsa yelped as her arm was yanked into the tank all the way to the shoulder, slamming her head against BETI's flank. She struggled for a moment, gaining no traction. Then she began to scream.

"What? What is it?"

The uterus flexed and clenched hungrily around Elsa's arm, the action splashing more fluid out around their feet.

"*It's stinging!*"

Wrapping his arms around her waist, Clive hung from Elsa with his full weight. She cried out in pain, unable to pull away.

"No, don't, *don't!*"

"Hold on!" Clive dove beneath BETI for one more crack at its release valve, and with a pneumatic hiss, it suddenly disgorged its contents. The remaining amniotic fluid slapped the floor like a tidal wave and gushed through the floor's center drain. "Alright—now close your eyes."

"What?"

"CLOSE YOUR EYES!"

Elsa did as she was told, just as Clive swung an IV stand wheels first into BETI's observation window. To her surprise, it shattered like sugar glass. Some distant part of her marveled at the anomalous might of the chronically underweight punk who she playfully bullied about his physique. *This is like those stories you hear where a mother lifts a four-door sedan off her trapped child,* she thought. *They call it "hysterical strength", don't they? Clive is going to be a great mom.*

"Hold still."

As bolts of nauseating agony shot up Elsa's arm from her hand, which was quickly losing circulation, she was vaguely aware of the clattering of surgical instruments behind her. The next thing she heard was a disturbing squelch just before she tumbled back onto the floor. The blood rushed into her fingers, and she noticed a weird, sickly sweet smell. She looked up to see Clive with a scalpel clenched in his teeth as he rifled around in the punctured uterus with both hands. His face was smeared with a gelatinous substance the color of pond water. Finally, with a gut-wrenching, tearing sound, he ripped the uterus out of its sockets and flung it to the floor. Then, for the first time, they both saw it.

The newborn dangled from the upper uterine socket by its umbilical cord. It was nearly the size of the uterus itself and took the form of a monstrous spermatozoan made of wiry muscle and vascular tissue. It emitted a piercing screech as it thrashed in mid-air, causing it to spin like a big top rope dancer. The motion twisted the umbilical cord and splattered the couple with globs of the vernix caseosa that stained Clive's face.

Vernix for "varnish", caseosa for "cheese-like. *That's the gunk that makes that"new baby" smell*, mused the detached part of Elsa. She knew that its caramel-like aroma was supposed to help bond mother and child at birth.

It didn't seem to be working.

As the creature sped its gyration, the umbilical cord began to peel, then split, and suddenly snapped back like a rubber band, sending the massive tadpole whirling to the floor. Just like you'd twist an apple off a tree branch, the other Elsa thought as she watched it slither away. She didn't move. Couldn't. Shock? No. Something was seriously wrong. She was weakening and wheezing. Losing herself. Her hand tingled and throbbed, and her arm began to stiffen. An allergen? A neurotoxin? Something entirely new? Wonder how Joan Charot will market this stuff, whatever it is.

"Look out!"

Clive slammed a storage bin down over the escapee and weighed it down with a heavy water purifier. The captive beat its body against the walls of its prison, but the bin didn't budge. With the jailbreak quelled, Clive turned to Elsa. Her pupils were like pinpricks, her breaths came slower and shallower. He grasped her wrist and peeled off her tattered glove to find a grid of deep, weeping puncture wounds across the back of her hand. Then she began to seize.

"Oh, my god. Hang on, hang on—"

Stuffing a towel under Elsa's head, Clive rifled through drawers in a blind panic until his fist closed around an EpiPen. He plunged the needle through her jeans and into her thigh—and, miraculously, it did the trick. With merciful rapidity, her spasms ceased, and she returned to him. Clive held her head in his lap and wiped away the brittle foam that had collected in the corners of her mouth. He propped her against his chest, and they watched their wrathful creation writhe in its plastic pen. Its tail had found a crack in the lip and slithered out, feeling around for its lost victim. Protruding from the end of the glistening appendage was a long, sharp spine.

"What was that?" Elsa gasped.

Clive held her close. "A mistake."

"Do you think it's in pain?"

Clive gave Elsa's arm a light tap to rouse her from her sleep, or the performance thereof. He had been staring at the ceiling for hours. The dingy glow of the streetlights had come and gone, replaced by a shaft of early sunlight slanting across the foot of their bed. In his mind, though, it was still the night before. He kept seeing their primitive hybrid bashing itself against the walls of the glove box in the clean room where they'd left it. He could still hear the ceaseless shrieking that carried on even as they finally convinced themselves to give up and go home.

"What?" Elsa had lain beside him all night, stock still, in a passable imitation of sleep.

"It's not formed right."

Their bed was surrounded by avant-garde toys, ironic takes on iconic cartoons. A sleazy vinyl rat cast a knowing grin down on the couple from their headboard as a glowing, skull-faced rabbit the size of a toddler glared at them from atop a stack of artist monographs and unread manga. Along some of their spines, Clive could see exaggeratedly short, squat caricatures of popular characters; "super deformed" was the name for that cute, comical Japanese art style. As of last night, everything in his life had begun to seem super deformed.

"We don't know that."

He resumed his contemplation of the ceiling. Elsa was right, of course. What were they to expect? There was no precedent for this form of life. No beauty standards for it; no counting its little fingers and toes. But still, there were those stomach-churning *screams*. That couldn't be right.

Clive sat up.

"I'm going to kill it."

Suddenly Elsa was wide awake.

"Wait!" She gripped his elbow with her bandaged hand. "There's still a lot we can learn."

Clive froze. He was, above all else, a scientist. Knowledge, for the sake of knowing, was his calling. How could he argue with her? And yet, against his very nature, he wanted to. Maybe he was finally discovering his own boundaries, beyond which there were things that he definitely did not want to know.

"We can find out how close we came to...something sustainable."

Meaning they would have to find out how much, and for how long, the creature could suffer. He was sure that's what it was doing. It just wasn't possible for its urgent cries and violent convulsions to signify anything like contentment, curiosity, affection, or even boredom. And it wasn't merely lonely, or hungry. None of the other surviving products of their DNA mixology behaved like that. Something was deeply wrong.

"Clive. It's OK." Elsa held fast to his elbow, trying to make him face her. Even with his glance averted, he could feel her eyes burning into the side of his face. Pleading, encouraging. It was a look she deployed against Clive's doubt, fatigue, and other human foibles that seemed to be missing from Elsa's constitution. Normally he welcomed this, but now she was weaponizing it. "It's alright."

"It's not all right."

Wrenching himself from her grasp, he stood up decisively.

"It's *wrong*."

As they gloved up in the observation room, Clive stared through the window at the glove box in the middle of the clean room. It was peculiarly still; he had imagined it rocking on its casters, or possibly smashed to bits on the floor. Now he couldn't guess what was going on inside. If its occupant were awake and crying out for attention, they wouldn't be able to hear it on their side of the glass. If they were about to wake it up… He braced himself for an encore of that nerve-twisting noise.

"Do we have to do this?"

Elsa was still trying to penetrate his defenses with that practiced and pining look of hers. *Think of a brick wall, think of a brick wall.*

"You don't have to. I'll take care of it."

He heard her pass into the theater as he filled an instrument tray. She may as well have a final moment with it, even if he couldn't relate to whatever strange sentimentality she was feeling. He took a beat before following her in. She stood stock still before the glove box, peering into its clear plastic hood.

The room was eerily silent.

A bead of cold sweat slid down Clive's spine inside his PPE. The acoustics created by his filtration mask amplified his breathing to horror movie proportions as he approached Elsa, who remained ominously motionless.

"Jesus, I think it's dead!"

"What?" Encouraged by this possibility, Clive peered in over her shoulder. Sure enough, their patient looked quite deceased. Even when he tapped on the window, it lay unmoving on the floor of the glove box in its congealing, grey-brown juices.

"Here, hold this." Clive passed the instrument tray to Elsa, and took up a pair of long, slightly angled Jorgenson scissors—recalling, with some irony, that they were typically used for hysterectomies. He cautiously pushed his hand through one of the box's heavy rubber ports and felt it seal around his forearm. Steeling himself for an unpleasant surprise, he gave the body a couple of exploratory pokes with the scissors. He was profoundly relieved when it did not respond.

"Yep. I'll bag it," he said, passing the contaminated scissors to Elsa.

"Well," she sighed. "At least it's not in pain now."

"Yeah."

Clive didn't find her concession very convincing, but there was no need for I-told-you-so's at this point. Neither of them were having any fun. He returned to the observation room in search of a biohazard bag, giving Elsa another minute to mourn.

With Clive gone, the barometric pressure in the clean room seemed to drop. Now Elsa could at least have a closer look at the corpse without the weight of her partner's judgment bearing down on her. She could tell he didn't want either of them to get too friendly with it, even after its untimely demise. Based on Clive's current attitude, Elsa wasn't sure if the future of this project was still the same as the day they left Joan Charot's office. They might have a very contentious conversation ahead of them, but she hoped that after a shower, a hot meal, and about twelve hours' sleep, she could make him see the light again. She'd never failed before and she certainly wouldn't now, not when it was this important.

As Elsa reached for the locks on the glove box, she noticed that they were slick with some foreign substance. Something that looked an awful lot like the unction that enveloped the body inside. She glanced around warily; nothing else seemed to be amiss. What was she even looking for? Steadying herself, she slowly lifted the hood, straining her senses for some minute sign of life. Using the scissors as a lever, she tried to turn the corpse on its back. It was slippery, much heavier than it looked, and its stiffening tail impeded a smooth rotation. When it finally flopped over, Elsa froze.

"It's empty."

She resisted the urge to try to rub her eyes through the goggles of her mask. The body looked as if it had simply erupted. Ragged flesh ringed a gaping hole through which Elsa could make out absolutely nothing. The murky ooze that coated the thing inside and out inhibited a clear view of whatever exploded structures might remain in there, but the casual impression was that of a total void.

Baffled, she closed the hood. What did this mean? With all that anatomic dead space, where had all that vim and vigor come from last night? Maybe this animal wasn't organized like a vertebrate, with a centralized nervous system; maybe it had a radial or diffuse neural net that ran along its whole body, like a hydra or a jellyfish. Hell, maybe it was meant to be in the water, and that's where their trouble began. Why hadn't they prepared themselves for such a thing? How could they have been so stupid?

Elsa was suddenly crushed under an avalanche of considerations that she and Clive had never made in all the time they'd been on this journey. In their desperation to prove Joan Charot wrong, and to strike while the iron was still hot, they'd rushed into things. Procedure had gone right out the window with Barlow's imaginary ethical concerns, leaving no reliable methodology to fall back on, no faithful Gavin to provide a fresh pair of eyes when they were mired in their own assumptions. Indeed, they had committed the worst of all sins: they had *assumed*. Their crime was not trespassing in God's domain. It was assuming that whatever they found there would be like them. They had just been projecting all this time, like any parent who expects a child to blindly follow in their footsteps. *OK. This is salvageable. We don't have to give up. We just have to start over with better questions this time. Less human-centric answers.*

As the locks clicked closed on the glove box hood, Elsa heard something else. A weird scurrying sound.

The pitter-patter of little feet?

"Clive?"

No reply came. Fine. OK. She hadn't slept, and she hadn't eaten anything but candy for who knows how long. All this new-mom stress was finally getting to her. At least now they could just go home.

BANG!

Elsa spun around in time to see an empty steel canister bouncing off the floor behind her. She held her breath, scanning the room for motion. *Not fine. Not OK. Not a corpse. A chrysalis. A cocoon.*

"Clive?" She raised her voice, knowing full well that he couldn't hear her. "CLIVE!"

She could see his back as he rummaged around in the understocked observation room for a bag, unaware of Elsa frantically waving her arms in his direction. She stopped dead when she heard a new sound. A *very* new sound. A simian chittering, slightly hoarse like the tortured shrieks of the night before. Slightly like Fred and Ginger's squeaky cooing, but bigger, more troublingly assertive. Elsa staggered backward into the center of the room, spinning on her heels in a desperate attempt to spot her company.

And then she nearly smacked right into it.

Whirling around, she found herself face to face with something hanging from the ceiling. Something that screamed with a primal rage before flinging itself from the overhanging pipes to the top of a storage rack, sending its contents flying. Elsa could barely track the blur of flesh and sinew as it catapulted itself across the room, turning everything in its path into shrapnel. Out of the corner of her eye, she saw Clive rush to the window.

"What happened?" He shouted.

He wouldn't hear Elsa speak the words he had once longed to hear—"IT'S ALIVE!"—but he could see it for himself.

"Oh, Jesus…"

Clive flung open the doors, but Elsa waved him off. "Don't! It'll get out!"

He retreated to the observation window, helplessly watching Elsa wheeling the glove box around in front of her as a body shield. Following her gaze along the path of destruction, he saw something rummaging around in a smashed-open biohazard container in the middle of the rubble. *It's searching for food,* he thought. *Looking for anything organic. At least it's not going for Elsa.*

Suddenly, the thing flew at her. She ducked just in time for it to ricochet off the wall behind her, splattering filth on impact and tumbling out of sight. Clive smashed the intercom button.

"Get out of there, I'm gonna gas it!"

"Wait!" They could both see its shivering shadow behind the boiler in the corner of the room. "Don't kill it."

"Elsa, get out! I'm hitting the gas."

To his immense consternation, Clive watched Elsa hunker down and creep slowly toward the little shape. He sucked in a sharp breath when it appeared to notice her. Inch by inch, it began to emerge from its hiding place. First, a pair of slender, fleshy antennae protruded into the light. They were attached to the end of a blunt snout over a rather feline split philtrum. Glistening strings of drool hung from its open maw.

"I'm not gonna hurt you…"

Elsa pressed forward as Clive exploded with anger.

"IN THREE! TWO! ONE!"

"Clive, I said *don't!*"

And to make her point, Elsa peeled off her mask. In that one single gesture, she offered her trust to the venomous being crouched in the darkness and shattered Clive's trust in her. Heartbreak would come later. For now, there was only terror and rage.

"Put your fucking mask back on! ELSA! Listen to me, goddammit, *you never listen to me!* Put your damn mask on, it's dangerous! Elsa, please—"

Clive watched in astonishment as she removed one latex glove and held out her bare, upturned palm.

"I'm not going to hurt you."

Finally, it stepped fully into the light. Its pale flesh was completely hairless, accentuating a curious pink cicatrice that bisected it vertically, most strongly along its skull. Dark, heavy-lidded eyes sat on opposite sides of its large, bobbling cranium, giving it an almost 360-degree field of vision—though for the moment it was focused entirely on Elsa. Behind its full, round cheekbones, tiny mouse-like ears quivered at the sound of her imploring voice. It gained courage, unfolding a hinged limb at the end of which hung a set of three clawed digits along with a thumb-like appendage. Elsa took this to be an arm until the creature came more fully into view. It had no forelimbs, only nubby little shoulders. Long, inverted legs descended from high-set hips on its truncated torso, and a short tail aided its balance. It was about the size of a large house cat, with an appearance somewhere between a rat and a rooster. It cocked its head back and forth on its flimsy-looking neck as it continued to evaluate Elsa's threat level.

With a sudden hop and a little squeal, it tiptoed toward her outstretched hand. She gazed into its strangely soulful eyes. It looked so vulnerable in the clinical light of the clean room. It shivered from excitement, or exposure, or both. It was probably cold, and hungry, too. Elsa knew what it was like to feel unsafe. She also knew that you felt safer when someone else made themselves unsafe along with you. The critter emitted a gentle, gurgling coo that Elsa gratefully recognized.

"It's imprinting," she whispered to herself.

In a strange imitation of Michelangelo's "God Creating Adam", the creature's little antennae touched Elsa's fingers, feeling the lines of her palm. Then it looked up into her face. She couldn't help but smile.

"You're really something, aren't you?"

But then, something changed. The hybrid reared back, hissing and growling at something over Elsa's shoulder—something that was now coming at it fast with an IV pole. Suddenly Clive was between them, brandishing the pole like a lion tamer and shoving Elsa back into the observation room.

"Come on, GET OUT! How about listening for once, huh?"

Clive hissed back at the bristling beast, who squealed in confusion as he slammed the door in its face.

"Are you crazy? Huh? Are you trying to get yourself killed?"

"I had the situation under control!"

"You had it under control? You're forgetting why we came here."

"You know what? We can't do that now!" Elsa spat.

She was amazed by his refusal to catch up with reality. Nothing was the same as they thought it was last night. If anything, the specimen was remarkably healthy. It wasn't some deformed county fair casualty—it was growing, gaining strength—but Clive had balked at its chrysalis phase like some hilljack rube. They had worked so long and hard to reach this very moment, but now her collaborator looked upon their achievement with fear and revulsion. Where was this coming from?

She pointed through the glass. "Look at it."

"What's that supposed to mean?"

Elsa rolled her eyes, exasperatedly. Fine, if he wanted to gas it, they'd gas it, but not the way he meant. "Let's just knock it out with some ether. Find out what we've got."

She turned the release valve, and somniferous gas flowed into the clean room. The creature snuffled the air in distress. It started to run in circles, finding nowhere to go. Elsa bit her lip, quashing any sign of emotion that Clive could use against her. She was the rational one here, after all. Their experiment would only be in vain if they failed to learn anything from it. Soon, the creature's orbit became slow and wobbly. It bonked into one obstacle after another until it collapsed to the floor. Finally, its little breaths were the only sign of life.

In their darkened radiology lab, Clive and Elsa got their first look at the inside of their creation.

The inaugural MRI scan was not the illuminating experience they had hoped for. Clive hunched over the computer, enlarging one image after another, ogling the creature's alien organs in disbelief. Fred and Ginger were simpler critters, rather like large grubs; whatever surprises their morphology offered rested safely in the context of their more recognizable features. Clive and Elsa had assumed that the addition of human ingredients to their cocktail would produce more predictably humanoid features. Instead…well, something else had happened.

"This is unbelievable. I don't even know what half of this is!"

"There must be some rogue elements. Junk genes pushing through," Elsa sighed as she crossed to the steel exam table where their still-unconscious subject lay curled on a surgical mat.

Its pale skin prickled with gooseflesh; just looking at it made her feel chilly, and she resisted the urge to pick it up and hold it. Clive arrived at her side with a still camera and clicked away as she palpated the end of its tail, collecting a droplet of the mystery toxin on a glass slide.

"Be careful with that!"

"It's some kind of self-defense mechanism," she mused, feeling inwardly relieved that the stinger hadn't turned out to be an ovipositor.

"Yeah, or attack venom," Clive grunted.

"None of her animal components have predatory characteristics," Elsa argued as she added the new slide to the queue next to the microscope.

"Well…there is the *human* element."

He had begun to detect a whiff of sentimentality in the way Elsa discussed H-50. The hybrid was technically female, with a discernible child-bearing infrastructure, but Clive sensed something suspiciously personal in Elsa's increasing use of "she" and "her". It was one thing for them to give their more primitive protein-producers names like Donny and Marie, or Brad and Angelina; most of them hadn't lived long enough to risk attachment formation, anyway. But the way Elsa handled H-50, and the intimate language she used, gave him pause. He made a point of reinforcing the word "it" in conversation to try to keep them grounded.

Clive added a new transparency to the negatoscope on the wall and studied the collection of blowups it illuminated. Some of H-50's organs were identifiable, based on common appearance or their apparent activity; others were uncanny, familiar yet obscure. Clive pointed to a set of smooth, bulbous masses in H-50's thoracic cavity.

"What are these?"

Elsa squinted. "Lungs?"

"No, *these* are the lungs."

"Tumors?"

Clive cast a skeptical glance over his shoulder at the sleeping hybrid. "Well, I guess we'll find out in the autopsy."

She squared up with him defiantly, but he wouldn't back down.

"Look, this wasn't supposed to go this far, OK? It wasn't even supposed to go to full term."

"*But it did.*"

Clive resisted the urge to raise his voice, something that he knew would only cause Elsa to shut down and shut him out. Maybe her own words would be more effective than his. "I'm sorry, but what happened to 'We're just gonna prove we can do it'?"

"So, what are you saying? You're really going to kill *it*? Hmm?" She nodded toward the vulnerable form. "You think you can do that?"

They watched the gentle rise and fall of its chest as it slept peacefully, oblivious to the harsh exam light shining down on it. Elsa woke up the monitor connected to the microscope and showed Clive what was happening on the current slide. His eyes grew wide.

"It's growing fast!"

An understatement. The cells were replicating wildly, quickly filling the screen. Clive couldn't disguise his admiration. Despite all his misgivings, they had created new life. A rather potent life.

"It's *aging* fast. Days within a matter of minutes."

"You think it's the Ambystoma gene?"

Clive was referring to the salamander material whose regenerative properties held particularly high hopes for their long-term pharmaceutical goals. It had innumerable applications, provided cell regeneration stayed within desirable limits.

"It might be," Elsa replied. "The point is, this thing is going to die soon, anyway. We're going to get to observe its entire life cycle in compressed time. We'll never get an opportunity like this again."

"…So it's dying."

"*She's* dying. All by herself."

This peculiar remark gave Clive a strange chill; a dark, premonitive sort of feeling. He watched Elsa out of the corner of his eye as she stared at their sedated subject. *Why would she say it like that?* She had been needling him with not-so-subtle emotional language to chip away at his desire to put H-50 out of their misery, but this was different. It wasn't aimed at him. Her mind was somewhere else as she gazed at the lonely animal on the slab, somewhere he couldn't follow. That wasn't strange in and of itself. He was used to her melancholy moods, though their source was a mystery. At first, he took it personally that she never let him in, but he had learned to focus on the ways she showed her trust in him. She never questioned his love for her, never tested his loyalty. Elsa's touch aversion extended to medical treatment; maybe she sympathized with the unwilling patient before them, who couldn't properly consent to their care. The little monster had no Fred to snuggle with after being poked and prodded all day, no Clive to hold her when she worried about things she couldn't name.

Suddenly, Clive was gripped by the urge to wrap his arms around Elsa, but he couldn't make himself cross the rift that now yawned open between them. Just as their dreams seemed to be coming true, they were fighting over…what exactly? What bothered him so much when they were making such incredible strides? The dark feeling still nagged at him, but he tried to stuff it back where it came from. Elsa was right. This would all be over soon, no matter what they did or didn't do, and what they stood to gain far outweighed the pains they took to get it. As he watched his partner grow ever more distant, he soothed himself with the thought that they would be home soon. *She's really one of a kind,* he thought. *They both are. I guess that counts for something.*

Gavin wound his way through the bustling clinic to where Clive hunched over the incubator. He didn't look up as the younger man handed him a pair of fresh vials, filled with blood from a very fussy Ginger. Gavin had only just begun to get used to the little monsters, who were not always as adorable as they were at their meet-cute on Fred's birthday. Their busy schedule of invasive tests and exams could make them downright ornery, and the stress was wearing on their relationship; they seemed to be getting on each other's nerves lately, on the increasingly rare occasions when they interacted.

Or maybe Gavin was projecting all this due to his own heightened stress levels. What started out as an exciting time for the brothers had quickly given way to confusion and drudgery, and to make matters worse, Gavin sensed that Clive bore some enormous burden that he would not share. The older man always had a somewhat anemic cast, which complimented his punk rock aesthetic, but lately he just looked exhausted. He still hadn't shed any light on this secret side project with Elsa, and his vaguery was worrisome in and of itself. If he was working on something exciting, then he should seem *excited*. Instead, he seemed haunted, irritable, anything but his usual calm, cool self. And he'd made himself so scarce. Even when Clive was physically present, Gavin couldn't be sure where his mind was.

Clive passed the vials back without turning around, and Gavin cleared his throat. "Hey, estrogen levels have been low these days."

Clive glanced up from under his unwashed forelocks. "What? How long?" This seemed to wake him up, though firmly on the wrong side of the bed. "What are you talking about? What do you mean 'these days'? Are you sure?"

"Of course!" Gavin resentfully. He brandished his ledger. "I did all the tests. Progesterone, testosterone, estradiol. It's all in the logs!"

Clive snatched the book out of his brother's hand and paged through it fretfully. "I'm sorry. I've had a, um… I'm a little worn out."

Gavin stowed the vials, then turned back around to find Clive gazing vacantly toward the ventilation panel in the drop ceiling. He was completely motionless. It looked like he'd forgotten where he was. It gave Gavin the creeps.

"So uh, I guess that thing, that…experiment you got going on…you're still not ready to talk about it?" Gavin smiled artificially.

Clive pivoted slowly, scanning the busy clinic. In happier

times, the controlled chaos of this environment was energizing. The whole staff shared in the heroic feeling of working way out on the bleeding edge of their field, and Clive's optimism was infectious. The challenges they faced from financiers, regulators, competitors, public protests, and even their own astronomically high standards only fueled their collective drive to succeed. The lively cacophony of clanking instruments, chiming computers, and humming machinery was usually joined by Clive's offbeat mixtapes, cyberpunk soundtracks for their quest to save the world. Alongside his professional ambitions, Clive's secondary mission was to make science cool.

But lately, all that controlled chaos felt different. Uneasy. Oppressive. The clinic felt airless and claustrophobic; the crew unfocused with its iconoclastic leader physically and mentally absent. The ambient symphony had degenerated into plain old noise, and sounded even noisier than usual lately, as if some unseen gears were grinding away behind the walls. A muffled hissing, howling, or screeching could be heard, which Gavin accepted as a pissed-off printer somewhere in the bowels of the lab. Clive continued his scan for invisible enemies as his brother tried and failed to make eye contact. Suddenly, Clive snapped back to attention.

"Hey, how do you listen to this crap? What is this?"

Clive crossed to the stereo with a cagey grin. He cranked the volume on a marauding hardcore track, causing several lab assistants to WHOOP! and throw up devil horns. Maybe it gave them a brief glimpse of the old Clive, but up close, Gavin wasn't buying it. His brother's forced smile couldn't cover the hunted look in his eyes.

"What were you saying?" Clive asked, barely audible over the speakers.

"Nothing."

"Day seven."

Elsa spoke loudly and clearly into her digital dictaphone to beat the fracas in the clean room. Their specimen was making quite a racket today. She strained at the end of the leash they had tied to a 25 lbs. gas cylinder, emitting an unearthly expression of disapproval. Her vocal range was quickly expanding; the demonic scream with which she announced herself to the world was now joined by a suite of animal sounds that she somehow used in concert. A happy hybrid could make dolphin-like clicks and whistles along with a feline purring sound, but when displeased—which was usually—her rasping screeches were accompanied by a goat-like bleating in an auditory assault that made the two scientists reconsider their position on whether Hell was real. Clive worried constantly that the staff could hear her, and his anxiety amplified every burble and squeak from the air ducts to hallucinatory levels. And as H-50 grew bigger, she grew louder.

The creature was rapidly growing out of her construably cute infancy and into something more robust. Tough cables of muscle twitched on her chickenish legs, and she was developing the paunch of a tubby toddler. Dark veins stood out here and there on her pale, clammy skin, and her puppy dog eyes were habitually narrowed in a scornful scowl. As her head swelled, her antennae shrank down over her cat-like mouth; she may have had less use for those feelers now that arms had sprouted from her shoulders. These baby doll appendages were still fused to her trunk at the elbow, so she couldn't do much damage with her scrawny forearms and miniature hominid hands. But the day would soon come when she could put her opposable thumbs to work, and Clive was not looking forward to it. For now, he was more concerned with the venomous tail that had doubled in length. To contain her dreadful spine, they had capped it with a baby bottle, which she wielded like a club.

"We've got H-50 on a diet of chlorophyll, roughage, bean curd, and enriched starch," Elsa continued.

Without taking his eyes off the potentially deadly diner, Clive mixed up a fresh batch of the nutritious glop that was her only and least-favorite food. Hunching down, he moved in on the creature, menacing her with a turkey baster full of green sludge. He knew that comparisons to Dr. Frankenstein were in their future, but he never expected to feel as much like Igor as he did right then.

"You're gonna eat this. YOU'RE GONNA EAT THIS!"

H-50 lunged at him, and his feet left the ground. If only he could stop flinching. His frayed nerves could barely handle the sight of the creature. She was faster and stronger every day, and her movements were unpredictable. He imagined that he should be asserting dominance somehow, but he couldn't steady himself long enough to show her who was boss. He gripped the baster like a dagger and moved in for the kill once more, and the little ball of muscle exploded with a blood-curdling war cry. He gripped the mixing bowl until his knuckles hurt, fighting his fearful shaking.

"Just a little bit, please? Come on, *just a little—*"

Elsa watched with concern as he chased their subject around the cylinder. The heavy hunk of metal was bigger than H-50, but it ground against the floor as she yanked it this way and that. Soon she'd be strong enough to drag it around behind her, and then their lives would become a lot harder. They had to figure out the food problem, fast.

"She seems resistant to feeding," Elsa told the dictaphone, humbled by her own understatement, "though her rapid growth *should* generate a proportionate appetite."

"You're gonna eat it. Eat it! FUCK!"

The beast flung herself at Clive again, knocking into the bowl and splattering him with her lunch. That was it. He slapped the bowl and baster down on the floor and walked away, covering his ears with his soiled hands.

"Oh god, I can't take this thing anymore. This is impossible!"

H-50 wailed infernally and lurched forward hard enough to pull the cylinder over on its side. Her leash whipped her to the ground with a SMACK where she lay writhing on her back. Elsa watched her kicking her feet in a puddle of spilled slop, and wondered where the hell she got all this energy, if not from food. She found herself thinking about the Xenomorph from *Alien. What did that species eat? Nothing, I guess. They just fuck and kill.*

H-50's wretched yowling reminded Elsa of a sick barn cat, which gave her an idea. Grabbing a fresh surgical gown, she tossed it over the squirming hybrid and swaddled her. With only H-50's head protruding from the tight little bundle, all they had to do was get the food into her mouth. Elsa held on tight and pointed the creature's muzzle at Clive.

"Bring it over here."

Gritting his teeth, Clive cautiously steered the slimy airplane toward H-50's firmly shut hanger. They cooed and cajoled her as Elsa poked her fingers into the creature's cheeks to wedge open her jaw. *"Good girl!"* she sang as the baster went in. H-50's eyes rolled like spooked cattle as Clive emptied the entire baster down the hatch. As soon the cargo was successfully loaded in. She blew a huge raspberry, coating him in green slime.

"This isn't going to work." He stepped back, stifling violent impulses. This was turning into a scene from *The Exorcist*. H-50 squealed and belched more food onto her despairing waiters. "She makes too much noise. People are going to notice. And she *stinks!*"

Elsa furrowed her brow. Clive was right. The hybrid had developed an unpleasant teenage aroma that they couldn't bathe her fast enough to mask, and her messy meals weren't helping matters. With Clive out of her face, H-50 hiccuped and chittered happily to herself as Elsa stroked her bald head.

"We'll just feed her with a drip," she offered unconvincingly.

"How are you going to feed her with a drip? She's just going to rip it right out!"

Suddenly, H-50 wrenched herself from Elsa's grasp, tearing off a lab coat pocket and taking a box of Elsa's favorite candy with her to the ground—and then a discovery of immeasurable importance was made. The scientists watched in astonishment as H-50 sniffed at the scattered neon candies and, with a cheerful whistle, she began to hoover them up, stalking them across the floor like Pac-Man. Clive had a vision of the old board game Hungry Hungry Hippos, and the thought collided with the hippo-like cryptids on Elsa's candy box. H-50 was starting to look a lot like the mascot of her new favorite food, with her bulbous dome, protruding belly, and squat, powerful haunches. He would have laughed if he didn't feel like crying.

Seeing an opportunity, Elsa scooped up the surviving candies and quickly whisked them into the dregs of H-50's prepared slurry. The creature watched with intense interest. Cautiously, she padded toward Elsa's outstretched spoon, her little antennae scanning for signs of treachery.

"Come on. Try it!"

Elsa could hardly contain her excitement when H-50 began to drool…then suddenly plunged face-first into the bowl. Elsa looked at Clive, choking back tears of joy. He added a final memo to the dictaphone:

"Tracking her feeding habits, we've determined that the H-50 craves high-sucrose foodstuffs."

He watched in awe as Elsa gingerly wiped the corners of H-50's mouth before the creature dove back into the bowl. Clive had to admit that there was a beautiful sort of symmetry in this development; a delightful irony in the fact that their artificial offspring should share her techno-mother's sweet tooth. The thought also made him a little sad. The very night they brought this being into the world, moments before the blessed event, they were teasing each other about whether to have a child. He couldn't bring himself to tell Elsa exactly how badly he wanted to become a father, how long the prime directive had been growing within him, making itself unignorable. He knew she would just razz him about his biological clock ticking and remind him that they had time to worry about all that later, and too much work to do now. But there she was, veritably glowing with pleasure as she nursed their happy little homunculus, and all he felt was this helplessness. This alienation. This mounting dread.

4

Clive slumped into a chair in Barlow's cramped Newstead Pharmaceuticals office. Neither he nor Elsa were ever that happy to see their project manager, but Barlow couldn't help but notice that there was something off about Clive tonight. His standard presentation was fashionably rough around the edges, but today he looked simply haggard. *Like someone who's been up all night with a screaming baby,* Barlow thought. *And she's not here... Could they hide something that big from me?* He brushed the thought away with the memory of Elsa's slender figure, something he usually tried to ignore.

"Elsa couldn't make it?"

"She's at the lab. Holding things together."

Clive spoke slowly, as if he were reading from a cue card. Barlow was never much of a mind-reader, but it seemed that there could be trouble in paradise. It occurred to him that this might be a good thing; if there were a schism brewing between the couple, he might be able to form an alliance with Clive. Barlow's life would be a lot easier if he could keep at least one of them in line.

"She's not very happy with the new directive, is she?"

"It was our facility," Clive parried. "We were supposed to have autonomy."

"I know. And I *am* sorry," Barlow insisted, leaning in conspiratorially. He fixed Clive with what he hoped was a sympathetic gaze. "The truth is, if we don't start projecting profits—*big profits*—soon, Newstead is in serious trouble!"

He waited for a reaction, but Clive just stared back emptily. Eerily. Barlow pressed on, searching for the words to activate him. "We need capitalization to move forward, which means that Phase 2 is not just an option: It's all we've got. If you guys don't hit a home run at the shareholders' presentation with Ginger and Fred…we might not even have that."

His naked desperation wasn't as inspiring as he hoped. Clive held him in that vacant stare, breathing shallowly through his mouth. Barlow was wondering if he might fall asleep where he sat when Clive finally replied.

"We won't let you down."

William Barlow was not reassured.

Elsa lay awake in bed, staring out the window at the streetlights. She'd rather be at the lab, but Clive had managed to convince her that it was important for H-50 to rest at least some of the time. Elsa had been with her all day and most of the evening, ditching out on the late meeting with Barlow. The only point of that was to ward him off anyway, to smile and nod as he harped on the importance of Fred and Ginger's debutante ball. As if they didn't know.

Clive lay still next to Elsa. She had feigned sleep when he eventually came home that night, hoping to avoid another fight, but he had collapsed from exhaustion. The mood between them had taken on an adversarial tone since H-50 came along. Elsa thought his anxiety should have been temporary considering their successes with the creature, but the bigger and healthier she grew, and the more they discovered about her, the less comfortable Clive became with the whole affair. Elsa couldn't figure him out—which was weird in and of itself. She was used to being the private one, the one who got to choose what she revealed and what she kept to herself. Clive was utterly transparent with her, maybe with everybody: a friendly, forthcoming, reasonably well-adjusted person. Elsa's hyper-alert disposition gave her x-ray vision with him, so this reversal of their usual dynamic was alarming. She didn't know where his newfound cynicism was coming from. They used to joke about the torch-wielding villagers who would storm the walls of the Nucleic Exchange Research + Development lab when they finally unveiled their power over life itself, but now Elsa sensed that Clive was switching sides on her. She just didn't understand why or how to fix it.

Maybe it's jealousy, she thought. That could spark such an unfamiliar attitude in her typically secure companion. He'd never had a reason to feel jealous of another man, but he might feel jealous of H-50. She enjoyed Fred and Ginger, but she never lost sight of their status as test subjects. It was different with their human hybrid. She was challenging to be sure, but she was also…kind of *fun*. They had something like chemistry. Where Clive was an obvious threat to the creature, radiating disapproval, Elsa was welcoming and sympathetic. H-50 would come to Elsa voluntarily, even allow herself to be held, and she knew that from Elsa came candy. Which Clive might call a bribe, but it had resolved their feeding problem, so who was he to complain? Still, it could chafe him that while Elsa had continuously refused to make a father out of him, suddenly she had this little being to raise and feed and cuddle. And H-50 was firmly a mamma's girl.

Elsa may not have been particularly maternal, but she found it easy to put herself in the creature's proverbial shoes. H-50 was hopelessly different from everyone around her; it held her back from what she wanted to do. No one listened when she expressed fear or outrage. They did not honor her boundaries. They did not want her to stand up for herself. She was expected to meet demands she hadn't agreed to, to be what others wanted her to be, rather than just being herself. But she wasn't all that hard to get along with if you only took the time to get to know her. All she needed was a little space, a little respect, and something sweet to eat.

Elsa knew what it was like to be different.

This thought dispelled all hope that sleep would come. She carefully slid out of bed and, assuring herself that Clive was undisturbed, tiptoed to the closet. Sitting on the floor under a canopy of clothing, she reached behind dusty storage boxes into a shadowy niche where her hands closed on a secret treasure: a well-worn, leather-bound case, roughly the size of a shoe box, with a raggedy old ribbon tied around its handle. It was adorned with peeling holographic stickers of rainbows and unicorns, and on the lid was scrawled a crude warning in blue magic marker:

My Stuff! - Private

The brass clasps clicked, and Elsa opened the box. There she found her own image. The old makeup kit had a mirror under the lid, and its pink satin upholstery cushioned Elsa's collection of childhood relics: colored pencils and crayons, picked-over sticker sheets, costume jewelry, and beloved toys. She took out a plastic tiara and rolled it between her palms, picturing how old she was when she last wore it. Replacing it, she then retrieved the most coveted of all her artifacts: a Barbie doll. Elsa stroked its long, golden hair and turned it over in her hands, trying to remember how it felt to move it around and bring it to life. The muscle memory of how to play with a doll did not return, but the feeling of the object itself had an incredible Proustian potency. The slight suppleness of its plastic flesh, the delicate definition of its fingers, and the freaky grinding sensation of its poseable knees had never failed to give Elsa an instant dopamine hit.

It wasn't that her childhood held such happy memories. Elsa was fiercely unsentimental and did not fetishize her youth, had no wish to relive a single second of it. What affected her was the feeling of *privacy*. As a child, she owned nothing. Not even herself. She was her mother's possession—a prop, an employee, a box to be checked. She was the carrier of her mother's genes and the steward of her burdensome estate, which now amounted to nothing more than a hoary old dairy farm, rotting way out on their abandoned rural acreage. Everything belonged to her mother. Elsa's time was not her own; the farm needed it. Elsa's body was not her own; energy wasted on fun robbed her mother of her usefulness. Elsa's gender, as far as her mother was concerned, was nothing but a potential distraction from her work. Men were never part of the plan. Elsa's father was seldom discussed by her mother, and to this day, Elsa never raised the subject even with herself.

Putting Barbie back, Elsa dug through the box until she found the single photograph she had retained from the past. Clive had never seen it. Neither had anyone else. Looking at it now, she wasn't sure why she kept it. Her mouth suddenly felt dry, and her palms grew cold at the sight of her young self in the firm grasp of her only parent. They were surrounded by virgin snow, the bare branches of an old oak veiling the blurry shape of the farmhouse behind them. Despite her hard-bitten asceticism, Elsa's mother was an attractive woman. She held her head high, and her regal cheekbones stood out against a brilliant cascade of long, flaxen hair. Her expression was one of not exactly affection, but pride. Her gloved hands gripped the shoulders of a little girl who could have been her clone: starkly blonde and fair, with large eyes that projected a strangely adult wariness. Elsa swallowed hard as a knot formed in the pit of her stomach.

Happiness was something of a taboo subject in Elsa's household. It wasn't *productive*, her mother might have said. She used her grim Scandinavian work ethic to protect herself from pleasures that might make her feel silly, vulnerable, or guilty. Elsa's box of treasures was important, was worth keeping all this time, for this very reason. It was her personal form of heresy. It was filled with things whose only purpose was pleasure. Things gifted to her by adults who took pity on her, like teachers and guidance counselors, or things she simply stole during their rare trips into town. The box itself was an illicit acquisition: a vanity set meant to hold everything a girl needed to become a woman. Elsa had acquired it during one of her archaeological expeditions into the attic. She was always looking for something her mother didn't want her to see—something personal or private, something that would make her mother more human to her. As it turned out, this was a tall order. On one occasion, she found a diary, and for a moment, she was filled with the impossible hope that it held the solution to a great mystery. But confoundingly, there was almost nothing inside. A few scant biographical notes added dutifully to dated pages, and then a white void, which Elsa found inexplicably chilling. She eased her disappointment by making off with the empty makeup kit, which had probably belonged to her grandmother—a nearly unknown figure in her life, little more than the dark silhouette far off in the distance of ancestral memory. It would be perfect for Elsa's heretical reliquary.

Even as Elsa outgrew the things inside the box, it remained symbolic of her independence, of her very survival. Elsa never let it go, not in college, not in grad school, not as a self-made woman striding toward a glorious future. It stood for her will, her ego, and, most importantly, her *privacy*. Her sovereignty. She had kept her secrets there her whole life. But now, it dawned on her that she had someone to share them with.

"In the first month since her birth, the H-50 continues to evolve rapidly. The emergence of arms, and the closing seam that bisects her body, suggest that she develops like a fetus outside the womb. Early cognitive recognition tests indicate growing intelligence. Still, her mind remains her greatest mystery."

Elsa's voice memo began Day 30 with the hybrid. She sat on the floor of the dimly lit observation room and watched H-50 navigate the latest puzzle. Between them lay sheets of paper featuring sketched silhouettes of various objects: building blocks, rubber balls, plastic letters and numbers, and other educational toys. One after another, H-50 matched each shape to its corresponding outline. In her newly proportional arms, she clutched a teddy bear (something Elsa couldn't help buying despite Clive's predictable protests) and headed for the right spot, clicking and whistling contentedly.

"Where does it go? Where does the bear go?"

H-50 padded along on her bird-like feet, the "thumb" acting as a kind of high heel, her tail swishing elegantly behind her. In another of Clive's least favorite developments, she wore a pretty blue dress meant for a five-year-old, which fit her just right for now. They had to keep her warm, and even Clive had to agree that it felt weird for her to run around naked, but he still cautioned Elsa against anthropomorphizing her. Elsa got where he was coming from, but wasn't H-50 at least a little anthropoid after all? She watched admiringly as the creature put the bear where it belonged.

"That's it, you got it again!" Elsa couldn't contain her excitement, even though it was clear by now that the exercise was beneath her precocious pupil. "You are such a *good girl*."

Elsa shook a handful of candies into her palm, and H-50 stuck out her hand with a broad grin, showing little white teeth. The vertical seam along her body wasn't entirely closed yet, but her early rodent-like appearance had given way to something distinctly human. Her face was becoming very mistakable for a human child's, which was handy for research purposes since it made even subtle emotions easier to read. H-50 shoveled a handful of candy into her mouth with a satisfied purr.

"You could do this all day, couldn't you?" Elsa said.

What she thought was, *Hell, I could do this all day!* She couldn't remember the last time she'd had so much fun. It didn't even feel like work anymore. She had to make a conscious effort to escalate H-50's tests so that they remained challenging, productive of useful data, and didn't just degenerate into pure play. Sometimes Elsa even wondered if H-50 weren't deliberately dragging out these easy tasks just to maintain a steady flow of tasty rewards. She was obviously getting smarter by the day, but had she reached the level of manipulating adults?

"I'm going to try something harder, OK?" Finding an empty spot on the floor, Elsa shook out a sack of Scrabble tiles. H-50 took immediate notice of the candy-like tiles clattering to the floor and awaited her new instructions. "So, *really concentrate.*"

Elsa picked out a set of four tiles and set them in sequence.

"E-L-S-A." She tapped her chest in a way that she hoped was meaningful. "Elsa!"

H-50 turned her head from side to side, pointing one eye and then the other at her instructor. She seemed to have a blind spot directly in front of her, like many animals with eyes set on opposite sides of their heads. Elsa had the urge to remind Clive that this was a common feature of prey animals and not predators, but she thought better of picking that fight, since this was a trend but not a rule. Besides which, there were other factors to consider: At a glance, H-50's eyes looked human, with an appealing hazel color. But on closer inspection, one saw that her pupils had a strange star-like shape. Typically, horizontal pupils belonged to prey, and vertical pupils to terrestrial predators, but there were many variances across the animal kingdom whose purpose was not well understood. As H-50 turned her head from side to side, Elsa continued to tap her chest.

"Show me 'Elsa'!"

Slowly, H-50 reached toward the letters…and scattered them with a disapproving grunt. Elsa scratched her head and sighed. Maybe this was too much, too soon; matching shapes wasn't exactly the same as grasping the association between symbols, sound, and meaning. And what was she trying to achieve, anyway? Elsa realized that she hadn't really thought this one through. She wanted H-50 to acknowledge the connection between word and object, but how was the creature supposed to do this exactly? She began to feel a little embarrassed. She wasn't a developmental psychologist. And they weren't meant to be teaching H-50, only observing.

But the hybrid wasn't done with the assignment. She fanned the tiles out before her, searching for something in the array. One after another, she arranged a new set of letters:

NERD

"Nerd?" Elsa blurted out in disbelief. Could this be some kind of bizarre coincidence? Or… She suddenly remembered what she was wearing: One of the print-on-demand tees she and Clive had made for their staff. It featured the Nucleic Exchange Research + Development logo: "NERD" in jauntily mismatching letters, along with a cartoon double helix wearing cool-guy shades. When Elsa tapped her chest for "me", H-50 saw the text on her shirt…*and read it.*

"Yeah! I'm a nerd!" Elsa blustered. "You made a connection! You are such a good girl! *Oh my God.*"

The hybrid responded with a smug grin and an outstretched palm, which Elsa happily filled with well-earned snacks. If H-50 could read, then someday they might be able to communicate. Their relationship was no longer one of scientist and experiment, or animal and trainer, but two beings sharing thoughts. Simple thoughts, to be sure, but this was still a radical development. Could H-50 learn to write, eventually? What were the implications of this discovery?

Their celebration was interrupted by Clive sneaking in like a thief. He scowled at the brightly colored obstacle course covering the floor. Ignoring the dark cloud hovering over his head, Elsa declared, "She did it!"

Clive looked around for witnesses as he carefully closed the door behind him. "What's going on?"

"She can associate!"

"Why is the cover off her tail?" H-50 retreated from Clive's judgmental stare to the safe shadows under a desk—her designated Time Out Place. "What's she doing in this room? You can't let her out!"

"What's the problem?" Elsa couldn't believe he wasn't even curious about what was going on with the Scrabble tiles. Working with the alphabet represented an obvious evolutionary leap, but Clive couldn't be bothered to ask.

"*What's the problem?* Specimens need to be contained." He gestured flailingly toward the clean room.

"Don't call her that!"

"What do you want me to call her?"

What Clive meant was, *Why do we have to call her anything? She is a specimen. She's not our friend. She's not our kid. H-50 is just fine.* But he instantly realized that Elsa was about to make him regret his rhetorical question. After a beat, she glanced at H-50's handiwork, upside-down and across from her.

"*Dren.* Her name is Dren!"

Dren cooed and clicked approvingly from the shadows, and Elsa glowed with self-satisfaction. Clive rubbed his face, gasping for air. *Ugh. Great.* Now H-50 had a name. Just like a real little girl, even if it wasn't a real name.

"Listen, you're talking to her like she's a…you're treating her like…" His own speech had become a minefield. Every word risked reinforcing the growing attachment between his colleague and their lab animal. "…a pet."

Yes, a *pet.* That seemed safe enough.

"I'm compiling a developmental profile," Elsa explained in

an officious tone. "She needs more stimulation than that one room."

"Oh, well, that's great," Clive grunted. "You know what Barlow said? They're renovating this entire wing tomorrow!"

Elsa's reaction to this disastrous news was not what he had hoped for. "OK, so we move her to the storage room downstairs. Nobody ever goes down there!"

"How do you know nobody goes down there?"

Suddenly, the couple were unloading weeks' worth of anger on one another. Neither of them noticed when, as their fight heated to a boiling point, Dren snuck away in search of a safer place to hide.

Gavin was pushing his restock cart down the hall toward the exam rooms when a disturbing sound caught his attention. Over the last month, he had learned to avoid the clean room where Fred first met Ginger, and its attached observation room. Not that anybody had given him new orders. It seemed like nobody told him much of anything anymore, but he discovered that this particular keypad had stopped taking the expected code. When he asked his brother about this, he was told to simply remove the room from his route; Clive and Elsa would take care of it from now on. Clearly, the couple was up to something, but Clive brushed away Gavin's questions with a confident wave of his hand. The older man always remained calm and cool even in the face of a heated argument, which was why it was so unsettling now to hear Clive shouting at Elsa, his voice shaking with anger.

"Your sarcasm's really gonna help when we get caught."

"We're not gonna get caught!"

"Caught?" That wasn't good. He couldn't make out everything they were saying, but this was a word he could not unhear. Clive and Elsa's project wasn't merely confidential. It was starting to sound illegal. He froze in place, stretching his senses to their limits. He had never violated his brother's privacy before, but this was a whole new world. Gavin simply had to know what was happening.

He reached into his pocket and produced a lock pick. He had picked it up in college for minor mischief purposes, but recently he had begun to carry it around again. He told himself that you never knew when a random power failure might leave you stuck on the wrong side of an electric lock, so it just made good sense to have such a thing on hand; however, solving whatever mystery lay beyond this specific door was the real reason he dug it out of storage.

"Yeah, breakthroughs come from risk… and go to jail… because of risks!"

Gavin struggled to keep his hands steady as he slid the pick behind the '6' key and carefully turned its angled head until it found the pad's emergency keyway. The mechanism made a cooperative *chirp*, and Gavin slipped into the narrow storage space between the hallway door and swinging double doors to the observation chamber. He held his breath and listened.

"So, you think they're going to renovate the storage room? What, they're gonna install state-of-the-art mop racks or something?"

"All they need to do is open the door! You're gonna risk our career on the fact that somebody won't open a goddamn door?"

Hiding was almost unnecessary; Clive and Elsa might not have noticed if he walked right in and stood in between them. The violence in the air made Gavin want to run screaming, but this could be his only chance to find out what was really going on. And perhaps, to save himself a prison sentence.

"It's the best idea I've got, OK? What else do you want me to say?"

"Why are we taking all these risks all of the sudden? I mean, what is going on?"

Gavin steeled himself for action. He might need to step in and side with the person who was *against* getting them all arrested. His heart hammered in his ears and his tongue had turned to sandpaper, but he knew he couldn't back out of this now. He told himself that he'd just collect a little more context, come up with a sane solution that worked for everyone, and then swoop in to save the day. Sure. A likely story.

"When did you get so fucking scared of everything?" Elsa spat viciously.

"When the fuck did *you* stop being a scientist?"

There, that oughta do it. There was no worse insult for Elsa, and Clive knew it. She would have to face the fact that she was being irrational, that she had let her perverted relationship with H-50 drag them off track, putting herself and everyone else in harm's way. She needed to remember what they were doing here in the first place. The sooner Elsa did that, the sooner they could get back to fulfilling their destiny as the saviors of humanity and bickering about whether to have a child. *Not whether, but "when"*, Clive corrected himself. *When* they would have a normal child, like a normal couple.

His moment of triumph was shattered by an ear-splitting scream as Gavin tumbled through the double doors into the observation room. His head hit the floor with a resounding *CRACK* as he fell on his back under the weight of a screeching Dren. She perched squarely on his chest, gripping his shoulders with shocking strength as he struggled to repel her. Her tail periscoped over her shoulders, its deadly spine seeking a clear shot at the intruder.

"No! Stop!" Elsa barked in a tone that Gavin would have found perplexingly parental if he'd had time to think about it. "You go to your place! GO!"

Dren looked over her shoulder at Elsa. From somewhere within her little body, she emitted a bizarre insectoid rattle. It was not a sound they heard often, and they didn't yet know how she made it, or why. A rattlesnake rattles to scare off larger enemies. It also rattles to distract prey before the kill.

At last, Dren sprang up and retreated to the shadows under the desk. Finally released, Gavin flipped himself over and scuttled backward toward the door. As he hauled himself to his feet, Clive and Elsa closed in on him.

"She won't hurt you!" Elsa promised absurdly.

Clive tried to put his hands on his brother, but primal fear still gripped Gavin's faculties. His eyes rolled in animal terror, and he waved his arms defensively before him as if he'd suddenly gone blind.

"Get away from me!" Gavin cried as he slipped through Clive's grasp and out of the room.

Clive held Elsa in a withering gaze. She bit her lower lip as she searched for her best defense.

"OK. So…we have to deal with this."

Clive and Elsa dollied a large cardboard box out of the elevator and down a darkened corridor in the lab's neglected basement. They wheeled their illicit freight around stepladders, broken printers and fax machines, and crates shrouded in plastic sheeting. As they hustled along, they searched the shadows for intruders while a curious whistling sound emanated from the box.

"It's OK Dren, it'll just be a minute, alright?" Elsa whispered as she shushed their restless passenger.

"I don't know about this!" Clive hissed.

"You got a better idea?"

Dren's whistle rose sharply into a frustrated squeal.

"You stop that!" Clive spat at the box. Dren's complaints only grew louder, and he shot Elsa a desperate look. "Go go go, open the door!"

Elsa sprinted ahead and swung open the doors of the storage room just as Dren's SOS reached a fever pitch. Dim fluorescent lights rattled to life as Clive closed the doors behind them. He stifled a sneeze as they wound their way through a dusty labyrinth of steel shelves. Obviously, Elsa was right that no one ever came down here, but he wouldn't be able to relax until he dealt with Gavin. Clive owed him a very big, very long explanation, he knew, but at least his brother wouldn't rat him out until they had a chance to talk. He thought. He hoped.

"I'm starting to feel like a criminal!"

"Scientists push boundaries. At least the important ones do," Elsa replied crisply. Clive was getting a little tired of this condescending refrain, and what it was supposed to imply about him.

"Sticking to a few rules isn't always such a bad idea either, you know."

"Nobody is going to care about a few rules after they see what we have made," Elsa chirped as she opened the box.

Dren allowed herself to be hoisted up, and she threw her arms around Elsa's neck. Clive cringed at the cloying scene. It was unnatural. Perverse. And worst of all, a distraction. Elsa Kast was supposed to become a modern-day Marie Curie, innovating historic tumor suppression treatments with her brilliant discoveries; instead, she was turning into the Jane fucking Goodall of mutant freaks.

"*'What we've made'*? Is that what you just said?"

"Yeah!"

"Nobody can see what we made!"

"Once they see Ginger and Fred, don't you think the world is going to want to know what's next? Do you think they could really look at *this face*," Elsa said, rubbing noses with Dren, "and see anything less than a miracle?"

Clive was starting to rethink his desire to make a mother out of Elsa. He shuddered inwardly at her soft, dopey affect, and the way she and Dren stared into each other's eyes as if they were the only two people in the room. Elsa's edge was melting away, and for what?

Suddenly, as if to express everything Clive was thinking and feeling, Dren vomited onto the floor in two violent jets.

"Oh, sweetie! Sweetie, you're sick, oh no!" Elsa comforted

Dren in a voice Clive had never imagined coming out of her mouth. To his horror, she carelessly wiped the hybrid's lips with the sleeve of her cardigan. He used to like that sweater a lot. She pressed the back of her hand to Dren's cheek and frowned. "Clive, she's really hot!"

Clive looked back at Elsa blankly, biting back his own nausea. He tossed her a dust cloth.

"I gotta talk to my brother."

He beat a hasty retreat, barely restraining himself from breaking into a run as Elsa sang sweetly to the unholy thing in her arms.

Clive sat across from Gavin in the cold light of the clinic kitchen, rubbing his hands together nervously. Neither of them had touched their cooling coffee. Gavin was angry. Surely the angriest he'd ever been in his entire life. He still hadn't fully grasped the recent sequence of events or their implications for the future. But he knew Clive and Elsa had put him in a bad spot. To put it mildly. Their worst-case scenario was much grimmer than professional disgrace, or jail time. He'd nearly been murdered by whatever-it-was in the clean room, and now his brother, the person he had loved and trusted more than anyone in the world, was delivering the worst pitch he'd ever heard. He stared unblinkingly over his folded hands and awaited an apology that he was beginning to think would never come.

"I know it's crazy. But I need your support on this!"

"Do you know what happens if you get caught?" Gavin spoke slowly and carefully like one would to a child. He couldn't believe he even had to say it. Again. "What am I supposed to do if you go to jail? Do you know what happens to this place, to everyone who depends on you? Did you ever think about them? About *me*?"

Gavin thumped his chest, underlining the very personal impact of this professional betrayal. Their usual power dynamic had been turned inside out; they both knew he was right, but the younger man couldn't even enjoy it. Clive twisted this way and that, nearly curling up in a ball, unable to face his brother. He had always considered himself to be responsible for Gavin. He was supposed to lead them toward a bright future. This was decidedly not that.

"I mean, did you think *at all*, or did you just do what *she* wanted?"

Gavin may as well have stabbed Clive with a knife. "It wasn't like that."

"You could have stopped it at any time."

Clive shrank smaller still under the crushing weight of his brother's judgment. Gavin had never seen him like this before, seen this naked weakness, this cowardice. This moral bankruptcy. His hero had evaporated right before his very eyes. After passing unscathed from a sunny childhood into an adulthood promising fortune and fame, Gavin had finally lost his innocence. He was going to stand his ground until the right thing happened: naturally, Clive would have to apologize. He would acknowledge his mistake, he would rebuke Elsa, he would stand up for his family and for his colleagues. He would make everything right again. It was the only option. The right thing to do. Gavin waited.

Clive said nothing.

"You could have just said *no* to her!"

Gavin waited longer still.

"Try it sometime."

Clive didn't even look up as Gavin walked out the door.

———

Clive pushed a mop across the floor of the storage room as Elsa anxiously monitored Dren's fever. He was amazed by how quickly he'd descended from science superstar to janitorial staff, but he certainly preferred this job to Elsa's. She hovered over a gurney where the squirming patient lay swaddled in surgical scrubs. The bundle emitted a disturbing mélange of animal sounds: the cries of a baby, the cockroach-like hiss, and that satanic bleating, all overlapping unnaturally. Clive didn't know how Dren did it, but he wished she would stop.

Elsa squinted at the thermometer. "It's 105! This is serious."

"You don't know that for sure."

"I *know*, OK? We have to do something!"

"What?" Clive grunted dismissively, letting the mop clatter to the floor. "What are we supposed to do?"

Dren coughed wetly, her nose and mouth coated in congealing mucus. With her all rolled up like a big cigar, Clive couldn't help thinking of the *Eraserhead* baby. He stifled a bitter laugh as he remembered its reluctant father saying to his deformed, poxy infant, *"Oh, you are sick!"*

"W-we have to take her somewhere!" Elsa was flailing, irrational with worry.

"What? That's crazy!"

"Well, then—do something!"

Clive gestured at their dungeon-like surroundings and shrugged sarcastically. "Like what? Give her a Tylenol?"

His rebuttal slid right off Elsa. Telling her off may have felt good, but it wasn't doing him any favors. Whether or not this absurd situation *should be* happening was beside the point; it *was* happening. They had to do something, and they had to do it together, much as he would prefer to walk out the door, pretend the whole sad affair had never taken place, and start life over somewhere else. He ran his fingers through his hair and expelled the breath he'd been holding.

"We're biochemists. We can handle this," he said, as much to himself as to his grotesque family.

"How?" Elsa cried as she struggled to soothe her ailing

ward. Dren's fussing rose into an agonized squeal. "Fuck, *how?!*"

Clive held steady. "What do you do for a fever?"

"...Cold bath!"

He blasted frigid water into the slop sink. It wasn't exactly clean, but it would have to do. He gripped the hose, willing the basin to fill faster as Dren croaked and shrieked. *Boy, is she going to hate this.*

"Shh, it's OK sweetie, come on—" Clive and Elsa unwrapped the unwilling creature, who suddenly seemed stronger than ever. "You got her? OK, it's OK..."

Gripping her tightly by the arms and legs, they plunged Dren into the icy bath. She unleashed an otherworldly wail that Clive was sure would bring the entire building down on their heads. She thrashed against her captors, dousing them in freezing water and threatening to break free—and then she began to seize and convulse. She coughed and wheezed, her tongue protruding from her mouth as her eyes rolled back in their sockets.

"Jesus, her passages are closing!" Elsa gasped in horror, clutching Dren's face. "She can't breathe, do something!"

"What? *What?!*"

"I DON'T KNOW!"

Clive was paralyzed. He watched helplessly as the love of his life crumbled over the monstrosity that had torn their happiness to pieces. Pity and loathing formed a noxious emulsion in his gut. A thousand thoughts raced through his mind, not the least of which was the persistent desire to escape.

"Uh...tracheotomy! In the lab—"

"There's no time!" Elsa cried. "Look at her, she's *dying!*"

Clive spun like a top, scanning the storage shelves for anything that could bring an end to this nightmare. He hated Elsa then, but he couldn't stand to fail her. He had already failed his brother, and he had long since failed himself.

"Dren, try to look at me. Look right at me! Good girl, good

girl," Elsa begged as Dren continued to suffocate. "Try to breathe. I want you to look at me. *Look right at me!*"

Elsa's voice grew muffled and distant in Clive's ears. Soon he couldn't even hear Dren's desperate splashing. His eyes went funny, and he was pleasantly deafened by the sound of his blood pulsing in his ears. *Oh, I see what's going on. I'm having a panic attack,* he thought, with all the emotion of a man realizing that his car needs an oil change. The world seemed to pull comfortingly away from him, as if he were falling into a deep, dark well. A sort of anesthetized clarity settled over him. *That's what it is. Panic. I just can't take this anymore. It's just going to have to stop, that's all. I'll just stop it. I know what to do.*

As if some outside force pulled his strings, Clive marched stiffly back to the slop sink. Calmly, he wrenched Dren from Elsa's grip and, holding her deadly tail firmly in his fist, he pushed her head under the water.

"What are you doing? Let her go!"

If Clive heard Elsa, he was unbothered. He hardly even noticed the brutal cold stinging his knuckles, or the desperate woman behind him, fighting him with all her might. Dren swung her fists and kicked her powerful legs, but nothing deterred Clive from holding her firmly to the floor of the sink. As the strength drained from her, he felt his own vitality return.

"Stop it, let her go! You're killing her!" Elsa pounded on his back and clawed at his arms, sobbing and begging for mercy. He paid her no mind, shoving her to the floor without losing control of Dren.

Bit by bit, the appendage in his hand went limp. A warm feeling of accomplishment spread through his veins as he saw the little body in the water grow perfectly still. Her eyes stood open, and her small white teeth showed through her slackening lips. She rested like a stone at the bottom of the sea.

Clive became dimly aware of Elsa hanging from his shoulders and weeping to break God's heart. His calm, capable counterpart was dissolved in grief. Outrage poured from her ragged throat. Her girlish features contorted unrecognizably. She grasped fistfuls of his jacket and she sagged against him as they gazed down at their motionless creation. Dren now looked right at home with the closet full of aborted specimens upstairs in the lab.

And then she took a breath.

Shock pricked them both as Dren's body quaked, belching up a glut of air bubbles. *A death rattle?* Her eyes rolled, looking around, blinking. Her mouth opened and closed as if to speak. More little bubbles came. She lay calmly on the floor of the basin, staring up at her saviors.

"Hey…she's breathing!" Elsa looked into Clive's face, tears still streaming down her cheeks.

"Those weren't tumors," he said. They both remembered the mysterious masses in her thoracic cavity. "She has amphibious lungs."

He spoke as if he were an expert on the subject. As if either of them had ever had the slightest idea of what the hell they were doing. Just like Elsa wanted, he'd taken a big risk, and it paid off. For her, anyway.

"You saved her!" She smiled at him for what felt like the first time in years, her eyes filled with fathomless gratitude. "…But how did you know?"

Clive blinked. His jaw worked, his hands gestured, and he made a series of expressions as if he were explaining something, calmly and rationally as always—yet he made not a sound.

Elsa's smile froze.

"You did know. Right?"

He blinked again.

"Yeah."

As Elsa's tears dried, something shifted. He could feel her x-ray stare powering up, seeking to penetrate his shields. Clive had to do something before it bored right through him. Before this darkness, this guilt, this profound sense of failure swallowed him up. He could only take so much of *that* in a single day.

"Anyway, we can't mess around anymore. We have to clean this place up, make it safe!" he offered supportively.

She nodded, though her eyes continued to burn through him. He forced himself not to look away. He prayed she wouldn't fight him. He'd done all the fighting he could do. He wouldn't stand up to interrogation.

"Yeah," she finally sighed. "I think we can do that."

Elsa had chosen to play along. Clive nearly collapsed under the wave of relief that struck him. As he smiled down at her, he had the bittersweet feeling of getting away with something. For now.

5

The far corner of the storage room had become a bright spot in a cavern of shadow and dust. Utility shelves were arranged like makeshift walls around a twin bed piled with blankets and throw pillows. A dim bedside lamp illuminated a friendly audience of teddy bears, sock monkeys, and rag dolls. They smiled down at the sleepy figure curled up between them. The bright bulb hanging from the ceiling was dampened by a craft paper mobile featuring cutouts of butterflies, flowers, and dragonflies. From a distance, the improvised bedroom looked like a sitcom set in the middle of a vast, dark sound stage.

"Sweetie, you have been *such* a good girl lately. I have something special for you!"

Elsa settled into the chair by the bed, wearing a solicitous grin. On her lap, she held the leather-bound makeup case containing the museum of her childhood. Dren peeked out of her covers curiously as the lid opened and, after a dramatic pause, Elsa produced her golden-haired former playmate. Dren's eyes widened as the Barbie appeared to wave at her; suddenly it was as if Elsa had never forgotten how to play with dolls.

"Hi, I'm Jenny! I like cute guys, fast cars, and funny little creatures like *you*."

Dren was transfixed as Elsa tenderly arranged Barbie's hair and stroked her face. The creature's other playthings resembled animals she'd never seen in real life, but this one was recognizably a person, and not a little like the fair, feminine Elsa herself.

"She was my secret friend. I wasn't allowed to have her, so I had to keep her hidden, just like you."

Elsa touched Dren's nose for emphasis, which dispelled the creature's shyness. A slender hand emerged from her blanket and its long, delicate fingers curled around the toy. Dren's hands were very nearly human, except that they had only three digits and an opposable thumb. Their elongated appearance made Elsa think of Marfan syndrome. She joked to herself that maybe Clive would like Dren more if she reminded him of Joey Ramone; maybe it was happening already, as tensions seemed to be easing lately.

Dren was changing all the time. In just a short while, she had taken on the appearance of a young woman of 14 or 15 years, save for her inverse knees and tail. Though her vertical seam was still faintly visible, and her eyes still sat too far apart to escape remark, she had become downright pretty. Where she had only a bony ridge before, her eyebrows had filled out into dark, smokey arcs over almond-shaped eyes that turned up impishly at the outer corners and were ringed with suety lashes. Her high, rounded cheekbones held a healthy glow, especially when she smiled, which was more and more often. As she grew taller, her baby fat had melted away, and her body took on a subtle pubescent curvature. Still, not a single hair grew from her scalp, nor the rest of her body. She stroked Barbie's streaming yellow mane with wonder.

As Elsa watched Dren examine the doll, she noticed a feeling of satisfaction growing from some primordial place deep within her. It wasn't the first time recently that she had detected this foreign sensation. For Elsa, happiness usually came from achievement—and especially from anything she achieved on her own. Her greatest pleasure was defying the expectations of people who thought they could treat her like a little girl, proving that she could accomplish what whole teams of men could not. Clive washer partner in all things, he even felt like an extension of herself in many ways, but she preferred to do things by and for herself whenever possible. But ironically, just as she had proven that she was competitive with (if not superior to) any man in her field, she coming to know an entirely new form of joy: one that wouldn't grow in isolation. As she looked down at her creation, Elsa realized that she was experiencing her own evolution. Something that had to do with sharing herself.

As Dren rested the doll beside her on the pillow, Elsa felt a tear come to her eye and choked it back. She wouldn't want to unsettle the creature just as she was falling asleep. She stood up, leaving the makeup case on the nightstand.

"Good night, sweetie."

Elsa drew the curtains they'd installed around Dren's personal space and turned to her exhausted companion. Clive lounged on the couch they'd brought down after hours, which had become their bed most nights. Though Dren was maturing behaviorally as well as physically, it still felt unsafe to leave her alone for long. Their rolling slumber party could be kind of fun at times, but it was also enervating with its lack of sunlight, fresh air, and a firm mattress. Clive finished scribbling the day's final notes in his ledger as Elsa collapsed beside him.

"She's had a big day. She's going to be out like a light," she whispered.

Clive stroked her knee limply; it was all he could muster. They stared at each other in silence. For a while there, exhaustion had become the enemy of the relationship. As they moonlighted on Joan Charot's Phase 2 and Dren's upbringing, they rarely had the energy left over for kindness or patience. Whatever strength they could spare was eaten up by their ongoing feud over what to do with their illicit offspring. But as Dren had grown up into someone more manageable, Clive slowly and cautiously accepted his fate. Peace had returned.

Clive studied Elsa's face with pleasure. As the day's tension drained away, it left behind an uncharacteristic openness and vulnerability he found deeply touching. As Dren grew and changed, something was changing inside of Elsa. Something very deep. The irritating puppy love with which she had first embraced Dren had passed, making way for something more resolved and mature. The emerging Elsa was both soft and strong, focused, but without that rapacious edge she used to carry all the time. Clive felt like he was falling in love with her all over again.

They both watched his fingers trail up and down her thigh, and he was struck by a sudden flush of self-awareness that made him feel like an awkward teenager. It was not unwelcome.

"It's been a long time," he said shyly.

"My god, I didn't even notice," she giggled. "Is that what happens?"

"To couples when they…?" He chose not to add, *raise a mutant tween.*

"When they work too hard?" She cut him off with a coy grin.

"Yeah."

They laughed. Despite his profound fatigue, he found himself getting his hopes up. *Not that this is the time or the place,* he thought soberly, with the dozing hybrid only feet away. But before reason could prevail, Elsa was straddling him, her hair falling around his face.

"Hey," she sighed. It gave him a funny feeling, as if he'd just picked her up from the airport. *Welcome back.*

"Hi there."

She kissed him passionately, and something inside him unraveled. All thoughts of proper time and place vanished as she gripped the back of the couch, pressing herself against him urgently. He reached for her belt buckle.

"What do we have here…"

She stood between his knees and slid her pants down to her ankles, stepping out of them as she unzipped his fly. He shuddered involuntarily, overwhelmed by an ancient, juvenile fear that he wouldn't make it to the finish line. It occurred to him that they probably hadn't been so spontaneous since their courtship phase.

"We have to be quiet," she purred, enjoying his obvious turmoil.

"I…w-we don't have any, um…"

"What's the worst that could happen?" Elsa smiled, repeating back to him his own words from the night Dren came.

His heart skipped a beat. Before he could ask if she really meant it, she had taken him all the way inside of her. The shocking sensation of her naked flesh nearly concluded their reunion right then and there, but Clive knew that if he ever wanted another shot at this, he had to make it worth her while. Grasping her shoulders, he took control of their rhythm. To his shock and awe, she was letting go like she never had before. Elsa knew how attractive she was, and she had a command of certain porny theatrics that always swung the power dynamic in her favor, but all that artifice was gone now. Nothing was left but instinct. Intimacy. Their union was so natural, so complete, that Clive had the dawning realization that they were going to climax together.

And then he saw it.

Elsa had left the light on in Dren's room, and a lithe shadow appeared across the gauzy curtains around her bed. She was watching them. Clive stared back in horror. The dark shape grew closer and closer as his lover rode him to the point of no return. Elsa gasped as she gripped him in a series of spasms, and he shook with his own unstoppable orgasm as his eyes were locked helplessly onto the silhouette of the unnatural nymph tilting her head from side to side like an inquisitive animal. He shut his eyes against the sight, shame and disgust stealing the long-awaited catharsis from him.

When he opened them again, the shadow was gone.

"Here is a couple unlike any other we have seen before!"

Joan Charot's smokey, accented alto echoed out over the black-tie crowd filling the convention center. A spotlight picked out her crisp figure at a translucent podium on one side of the stage; she was impeccably groomed as always, projecting her aura of visionary wisdom. The anticipation in the air was something one could almost smell, a pheromonal undercurrent slipping through the strains of perfume, cologne, and fine wine that swirled around the hungry crowd of potential investors. The suspense was amplified by two screens hovering over the stage, bearing the sharp red Newstead Pharmaceuticals logo in the corner of a live feed of *something* that remained in shadow. On each screen, a quivering, organic shape just barely stood out against the darkness.

"That they are completely unique in the world is more than just fate. More than just luck. It is...by design!"

Joan Charot pointed a painted nail at center stage like God creating light, and spotlights struck a large, clear tank. The screens blazed with the illuminated images of Fred and Ginger, kept in their corners by plastic barriers. A chyron under each creature read AMRONUS ATTICUM—a deliberately obscure taxonomy, per Clive and Elsa's prerogative to keep their recipe secret—followed by AKA GINGER, FEMALE and AKA FRED, MALE. The dueling displays had a pro wrestling-style flair that reminded the couple of some gruesome internet videos they'd seen under the title *Japanese Bug-Fights*. Hopefully, tonight's demonstration wouldn't be as disturbing as the "Giant

Centipede vs. Deathstalker Scorpion" episode that had given Clive nightmares.

The crowd gasped in astonishment as flashes burst in the press gallery, but happily, no one recoiled from the sight of the bizarre duo magnified by the video feed. Fred and Ginger were looking pretty weird these days; no longer wiggly little grub-like juveniles, they were bigger now, and tougher-looking. Elsa thought they looked like large, predatory oysters, an idea that she promised Clive she wouldn't put in anyone else's mind. They bristled visibly under the bright, hot lights, and the sounds, sights, and smells of the roiling audience weren't doing much for their mood. Their proud parents only hoped that once the barriers retracted and they saw each other again, they wouldn't be struck with a bout of performance anxiety.

"Now let me present to you the minds behind the design…"

It was showtime. Standing in the wings, Elsa was champing at the bit to take the stage, while Clive might have run and hid as soon as he heard his name. He had been quaking with fear since he woke up that morning. When Elsa asked about his shaking hands and wan complexion, he blamed the fact that they'd been living like fugitives for so long that being back in the spotlight felt downright dangerous. That was fair; increased scrutiny could let a certain illegal cat out of its underground bag. But something else was bothering him, too, that he couldn't share. The doomed feeling that had dogged Clive from the moment of Dren's conception had arrived with him on the red carpet, hanging over his head as he and Elsa rubbed elbows with legions of future funders. After his scientific genius, Clive's greatest asset was the air of effortless self-assurance that compelled people to hop on his personal bandwagon. Tonight, he found himself ducking behind his diminutive co-conspirator as they met their growing fan club, and furtively wiping damp palms on his slacks between handshakes.

Mercifully, Elsa had enough confidence for them both. She virtually glowed in her white-on-white suit as she seduced the press and public alike, making all the world an offer it couldn't refuse. If things had turned out differently, Clive would have been overwhelmed with desire for her. After their inevitable triumph, they would have drenched each other in champagne and fucked like rabbits until the break of dawn. Now all he felt was this metastasizing dread.

Vibrating with excitement, Elsa grinned at her nervous partner, trying to inject him with her boundless energy. She straightened the silver tie he wore with the black-and-gunmetal tux that she had assured him a thousand times was the right choice. Whether he believed her or not, there was no turning back now. The future was calling.

"Splice masters extraordinaire: Clive Nicoli and Elsa Kast!"

Joan Charot swung her arm toward the couple, and a spotlight followed. As it tracked them across the stage to a podium opposite Joan's, they were blinded by camera flashes and deafened by the roar of the crowd. Giant banners bearing the Newstead Pharmaceuticals logo and slogan—DESIGNING A BETTER TODAY—exaggerated the image of conquering heroes bringing news of their epic victory over nature itself. Yet, it was clear that Clive would rather be anywhere else. Even Barlow looked more at home in his own skin that evening, tucked behind the curtain with Gavin and the other technicians, who were ready to lower the tank's barriers and monitor the grand affair.

Gavin. They hadn't had much time to talk that night, which was perhaps for the best. Clive's brother had congratulated him appropriately, greeting him with a firm handshake and a supportive smile, but Clive knew what lay behind it. Gavin had resigned himself to his fate, whatever it may be, choosing to put his relationship with his brother before the attractive prospect of blowing the whistle. But that didn't mean he was happy about it. Their relationship would never be the same, and there was one less source of comfort in Clive's world. He felt like a fool, performing like a trained ape in front of someone who knew his darkest, dirtiest secret.

"Uh, thank you. Thank you very much," Clive uttered, wringing his clammy hands. He fixed a frozen smile on his face and dove into their script. "Well, there's been a lot of talk tonight about advancements in multi-species morphogens. We've talked about our new protein-based compounds...um... disease-fighting agents for livestock..."

Elsa nudged him mercifully out of the way. "And that's all very exciting for everyone at Newstead. But let's be honest," she intoned slyly. "What's exciting for you people here tonight is to see these two creatures, alive and in the flesh!"

Excited whispers rippled through the house as inside the tank, the barriers slowly retracted, and Fred and Ginger spotted each other. Their snouts sucked at the air, and their flesh prickled with a tension that an innocent bystander had no way of interpreting. For the audience's part, they simply smelled money.

"These are state-of-the art, designer organisms; the first of their kind. The origin of a species."

Fred and Ginger clamored over the descending barriers toward one another. Each animal reared up stiffly in what no one but Clive and Elsa could know was a display of aggression. Drunk on her own charisma, Elsa pressed on with their commencement speech.

"Male and female. Like Adam and Eve—"

Audible only from the stage was a sputtering hiss that was definitely not part of the creatures' love language. Clive glanced nervously over his shoulder at the situation escalating in the tank. Something was deeply wrong. He whispered as loudly as he could into the wings, *"Raise the barriers!"* No one heeded him. All eyes were locked on Fred and Ginger, dewy with ignorant wonder.

"—coming together to enact nature's timeless story of love!"

The pair circled each other like delinquents in a knife fight.

Stretching upright, they began their peristaltic undulations—but this time, instead of the delicate fern-like tendrils, each one produced a sharp, black spine.

In a single instant, everything changed forever.

A collective gasp of shock shot through the air as the creatures pierced each other's flesh. Loud, wet punctures preceded violent jets of blood that painted the walls of the tank. The press surged forward as waves of investors scrambled to their feet, torn between the urge to flee and the inability to look away as Fred and Ginger's coming-out party exploded into an orgy of violence. Elsa turned around just in time to see something that made no sense to her: The tank was like a juicer full of fresh offal. As the melee intensified, the tank spiderwebbed and rocked on its stand, tearing out of its moorings. In the blink of an eye, the whole apparatus crashed to the stage, sending a shower of sparks, broken glass, and hot gore spraying out over the VIPs in the splash zone.

In the pandemonium that ensued, as blood-drenched business elites trampled each other on the way to the doors, relentless camera flashes joined the spotlights in their stark illumination of the sudden and highly public demise of the Nucleic Exchange Research + Development lab's valiant quest to save the world. At center stage, now ground zero for one of the most horrific science scandals since thalidomide, lay the deflating corpses of humanity's fallen saviors, still bleeding out amid the carnage of their own mutually assured destruction.

Or, at least, Clive had hoped that this event would nail shut the coffin on NERD. After this outrageous humiliation, he never wanted to set foot in the lab—perhaps any lab—ever again. But it was not to be so easy.

He and Elsa stood forlornly before Joan Charot to avoid getting blood on the upholstered seating in her shadowy boardroom. The space's dramatic grandeur had previously filled the couple with the pleasure of being welcomed into the big time, but now it felt hostile and frightening. They had been demoted from guests of honor to trespassers, and they couldn't have been less comfortable if they'd been clapped in the stocks. At least stocks would have felt appropriate. The dark radiation pouring out of Newstead's COO was only inflamed by Barlow's attempts to defuse the situation.

"Well, I think we all have to agree that this is a setback in terms of how—"

"It's a fucking disaster." As Joan Charot turned her gaze on Clive and Elsa, the air thickened in their lungs. "What happened?"

Clive swallowed so hard he was sure it was audible in the still air of their execution chamber. "Well...it was difficult to examine the remains, but um... It seems that Ginger has undergone certain...uh..." He yanked at his blood-spattered tie, which seemed to be tightening on its own.

"Hormonal changes," Elsa contributed.

"*Hormonal changes?*"

"She turned into a male," she spat out in defeat. The viscera and the thick, metallic stench that clung to her formerly white suit had stolen her last shreds of dignity.

Joan turned to their senior project manager, who nearly ducked when her eyes fell on him. For a moment, he just sat there gulping air.

"What? Just like that? Just *changed sex?*" he sputtered. "How can this happen?"

Gavin's voice echoed in Clive's mind: *Estrogen levels have been low these days.* He was so glad his brother wasn't here to participate in this grim postmortem.

"We really don't know. But clearly, two males caged together and stressed is..." Clive washed down whatever he was about to say with a swig from his water glass, which he clutched so tightly it might shatter.

"So, your first living hybrid changes sex, and you didn't notice?" Joan summarized sharply, slicing the air between them with her manicured nails. "How is that possible?"

"We can recreate them," Elsa offered, knowing full well that it wasn't an answer to the question. The actual answer was unspeakable. "No reason not to start over."

Joan slammed her open palm down on the table. Clive was sure that his feet had left the ground.

"No. More. Monsters." Clive and Elsa squirmed like their late specimens as Joan stared them down. "We don't have time for that. We need the gene that produces CD356, and we need it now."

CD356. Right, of course. They'd almost forgotten all about the protein whose discovery was the entire point of Phase 2. They could have been noses-down on that task still, while they were putting on the glorified donkey show that had just gone so hideously wrong. The flashy pageant had seemed like a good idea at the time, with Barlow nipping at their heels about Newstead's much-needed cash infusion. Now it was nothing more than an obvious strain on a team that was already spread too thin between the job they were supposed to be doing and the forbidden experiment they were actually focused on. And the real reason they were spread so thin must remain hidden at all costs. Blaming Barlow was tempting, but it would not have saved them.

"Do you understand?"

The look in their eyes satisfied Joan Charot that she had made her point.

———

"We have to get it out of here."

Gavin leaned against a support beam in the basement, his arms folded across his chest. If Clive resented their situation, his ire came nowhere near that of his younger brother, who truly did not ask for what was now happening to him.

"And take her where?" Clive asked morosely.

He cringed at his own response, or lack thereof. Everything he said these days dripped with defeat, even though they were far past the point where quitting was even possible. Worse still, he realized he had come over to Elsa's side of the pronoun debate; he hadn't even noticed this development before Gavin arrived to reinstate the all-important *it*. Clive turned away in embarrassment, but his brother wouldn't be ignored.

"Barlow is taking over every inch of this place, man. He'll find it!"

Dren lay on the couch, cocooned in a blanket with her favorite teddy bear. She rested her head in Elsa's lap and anxiously watched the two men bicker. Her verbal comprehension was still limited, but her furrowing brow and quivering lip said that she knew what was afoot. None of this was her fault, and yet somehow, all of it was.

"We gotta find some place, like, away from...everything!" Clive groaned, gesturing aimlessly.

He was coming to hate the sound of his own voice. To even say such a thing in their urban environment, on their limited budget, was as good as saying *Let's just stop trying. Let's leave Dren in a bassinet on the steps of the nearest Humane Society and pretend the whole thing never happened.*

"What am I not getting here?" Gavin exploded. "What did you expect when you made *it*? Didn't you have a plan?"

Clive's guilt and shame were obliterated by mindless rage. He stuck his finger in the younger man's face, his voice rising quickly to a shout. "Listen, little brother. We wouldn't be in this mess if you'd been paying enough attention to observe a *fucking gender change!*"

Of course, none of this was on Gavin. He'd been abandoned while Clive and Elsa played their twisted game of house, and forced to forge ahead on his own without any idea of the bigger picture, or the real risks involved. But Clive's pent-up indignation had reached critical mass, and it had to go somewhere. Maybe he couldn't dominate Elsa, but there was still the evergreen path of least resistance. His anger poured like lava onto the baby brother who once idolized him.

"And where were you, maestro?" Gavin bit back. "I was playing catch-up with all the work *you* weren't doing!"

"All you had to do was track some data—"

As the fight reached its boiling point, the two men failed to notice another voice joining the fray. Its calm, rational tone struggled to gain traction in the chaotic fracas, but it did not waver, did not give in. It turned up a notch, then two, then ten. At last it broke through, ringing out with crystalline clarity.

"I know a place we can take her!"

The Nicoli brothers fell silent and turned toward Elsa. Finally, someone was proposing a solution.

"All these years you've owned this farm, and you never mentioned it?"

Clive wheeled the humming, cooing cardboard box down the basement hall to the freight elevator. It felt like he'd done this very thing only yesterday, yet now they needed a much bigger container. Elsa staved off ahead of him, as much to act as lookout as to avoid his simmering ire.

"You knew I grew up on a farm," she replied tersely, picking up her pace. If Clive had been any less intoxicated by his own anger, he would have noticed a strange stiffness in Elsa's walk, and a growing distance in her tone.

"I didn't know you still had it!"

"It's not my farm. It was *hers*."

Elsa shot him a look whose deadly payload missed him entirely. Self-pity stopped him from asking *why* his beloved partner had never mentioned such an ideal hiding place for their hot property. One that wasn't subject to eavesdropping, interloping, or renovations. A place whose locks they wouldn't have to recode on a daily basis. Hell, a place with their own bedroom. If Clive had been able to ask why the farm remained a secret, he might also have wondered why Elsa spoke of her own mother like that, with icicles on her breath. As far as he was concerned, it was her exciting new way of annoying him. Anger had killed his curiosity.

"She's dead!"

"So is the farm."

What was that supposed to mean? What did it have to do with them? Clive wasn't in the mood for cryptic remarks, and he clammed up as Elsa swung open the rear doors of their rented van. The two of them dug their fingers under the whistling box and slid the 120-pound load into the vehicle. Before they closed her in, Elsa reassured their precious cargo.

"It's alright, sweetie. We'll have you out in a minute, OK?"

6

———

"You know, you can talk to me about your mother."

Dren heard the voice of the Male somewhere nearby. He hadn't gone far, but it sounded like he was on the other side of a wall. Confusing. Where were the Others? Where was *she?* Were they going somewhere together…or apart? At least she still had Teddy. The Female had spoken softly to Dren and let her take her toy into the box, so she knew she wasn't being punished. She tried not to be scared. She curled up around Teddy with her face against her knees and her legs folded beneath her like a bird's. She wrapped her arms and tail around herself and gave herself a soothing squeeze.

This was the latest in a series of boxes that Dren had been stuffed into. The Others would put her into a box in one place, and when they opened it up again, she would be in a whole new place. Sometimes the new place was nicer, like the room full of soft things like Teddy to squeeze when she was alone. More often, the place was not so nice, full of needles and bright lights and loud machines. She felt around inside the new box. There was a little slot before and behind her, but no light came in. She could stick her fingers or her tail through the holes, but she didn't know what was out there in the dark. The walls of the box flexed slightly when she leaned against them. She could smash through them if she really wanted to, but it was better to wait and see what happened.

Dren had learned lots of things in her short life, but the most important one was *patience*. She learned to do things that made no sense to her. She was taught to hide, though she didn't know from what, and she never knew for how long. She learned to sit still while the Others stuck her with needles that pushed something in or pulled something out of her. She knew to be quiet while the Others shouted at each other so viciously she thought they might bite each other. If she was good while these things happened, the Female would speak softly to her, touch her gently, and fill her hand with sweet, colorful treats. Dren found out that even the worst things had an *end*.

The end was a very important concept for Dren. Before and after were hard to understand. The only thing any living being could ever directly experience was now. Because of this, now was the same thing as forever. And when now involved pain or fear or loneliness, it was intolerable; unhappiness became eternal. But, with careful observation, Dren learned about change. Nothing was truly forever, and there were patterns to the changes. In fact, the scarier one now was, the more likely it was that the next now would bring treats and kind words and soft touches. Being patient, and doing what the Others wanted, could make a different now come faster.

Patterns helped Dren learn patience. The clock on the wall did not mean much to her, but there were *times* in her day. She learned to feel the different times coming in her gut. There were feeding times when she didn't even have to do tricks to get treats. There were times for fun games, times for scary tests, and finally bedtime—which she liked so long as she was good and tired. Otherwise, she might feel lonesome. But even when the Others left her all alone, there was plenty of time to practice the all-important skill of waiting. Waiting was a lot harder than crying, screaming, and fighting, but it had become her most important power. It was the main thing that brought along a new *now*.

Dren heard the Male changing his voice. He had been yelling and screaming at the Other Male, the weak one. That one wouldn't even look at Dren. He only shook his fingers in her direction, but he always seemed ready to run or strike. It made him seem unpredictable; a quality Dren did not like. He was probably still mad about her chasing him out of one of the rooms; she still didn't understand why she got in trouble for that. They were all so intent on keeping her *in*, and keeping everything else *out*, why shouldn't she defend their territory? Life with the Others could be very confusing, and the Males were always very angry about something. Now the strong one was changing his voice. He was trying to get something from the Female. She sounded unhappy.

"I don't even want to think about her."

She didn't raise her voice, but Dren knew what her tone meant: I'm done. When the Female was done, the Male could not start her up again. She would not talk, would not smile, would not give nice touches, would not budge. She would only start back up when she felt like it. Dren knew how the Female felt, but Dren wasn't allowed to be done. She didn't get to make rules, to give out treats or hold them back. She often felt mad and trapped. She thought she could probably hurt the Others if she wanted to. They outnumbered her, but they were slow, and they didn't seem very strong. Still, she stopped herself. After all, what would she do without them? The thing she really wanted was just a little respect. And something sweet to eat, to make it all worth her while.

The Male should just give the Female some treats, Dren thought in her abstract, sensorial way. Sugar was what made you want to be patient. Why didn't he think of that?

"I just want to understand!"

He was trying to sound gentle and nice, but Dren could tell he was faking. It seemed to her that the Male was often faking, except when he was shouting. The shouting was always real; the soft voice, only sometimes. Even when the Others kept their voices low, Dren could still tell when they were angry, or afraid. She could smell it. The Other Male especially produced a thick, bitter musk all the time, whether he was shouting or not. For now, Dren couldn't smell much of anything inside the strange new machine her box was in, which had a weird, oily, smoky kind of stench. Her head was starting to hurt from the odor and the stuffy air.

"If you could understand crazy, it wouldn't be crazy."

With a sudden roar, the machine began to rattle and shake. Dren's muscles seized with fear, and she braced herself against the flimsy walls of her box. It was extremely loud now and she could barely hear the Others, to tell if they were scared too. She wanted to scream, to rip the box to shreds and flee into the great unknown, but she held onto herself. She remembered the other machines she had been in, all the other loud noises that scared her out of her wits, and how she had learned to be brave. Had learned, with all her powers of concentration and courage, to wait. With a sad little whine that nobody heard, Dren curled herself tighter around Teddy, and practiced waiting.

———————

"It's OK, honey! There's nothing to be afraid of."

Dren was waking up. She wasn't sure exactly when, but the constant rumbling of the machine, with its dull roar and headachy fumes, had put her to sleep. The cold, too, had slowed her thinking and her muscles, slowly bringing everything to a halt. The sudden silence was as good as an explosion, shocking her back to consciousness before she even heard the Female's voice. How long was she asleep? Where was she? She tried to stretch her stiff limbs, bumping up against the walls of the box. There was a very long *now* before the doors of the machine opened and a dim light slipped into the holes, along with a blast of frigid air. She peeked through to see part of the Female's face.

"This is your new home now!"

Her happy tone didn't match her eyes. They were alert, wary. Should Dren be afraid? She tried to catch an informative scent from the Female, or the Male who arrived at their side, but suddenly there was just so much happening.

The Others pulled the box out of the machine and set it on the new ground. *Crunch.* There was something under the box, something crispy and brittle that made a sound under Dren's weight. The incredible chill poured into her nose and mouth, prickling her insides. When she breathed out, to her amazement, she could see her breath floating on the air. Her skin stood up in tiny points, as if pulled by a million invisible hooks, and she shook uncontrollably. When the Others opened the box, Dren wasn't sure if she still wanted to come out.

But the box was open, and Dren caught her first sight of the World. A vast blackness sprawled above her head; it was dark, but this was not the close, stuffy darkness of the places that she knew. Dren was used to walls and ceilings and shadowy little corners where she went when she was *bad*. This was…something else. The vast, empty dark that covered the World was shot through with dancing points of light that swirled around a huge, round shape from whence the cold illumination came. Was it an object, or was it a void?

The Others pried Dren out of the box and stood her on the ground. Her soft, gray nightgown provided no protection from the cold, and her feet were bare—their shape was so different from the Others that nothing of theirs would fit. Something bright and white covered the ground as far as Dren could see. She might have found it beautiful if it didn't sting the soles of her feet like needles as it crunched beneath her. She picked up one foot and then the other in a painful jig as the Others wrapped her in a thick, puffy blanket. The blanket itself was so cold she almost fought it off, but anything was better than plain air.

Gripping her elbows through the blanket, the Others began to guide Dren in a certain direction. The more she saw of the World, the less she understood. Great, dark, ragged-looking spires erupted from the frosty white ground and stretched high up into the air, many times Dren's height. From the darkness between these towers came startling new smells that frightened and attracted her all at once. There was something dank and damp that reminded Dren vaguely of the new foodstuffs she got when she grew out of eating that gross green goo—*Dren eats Plants*, the Female said, *not Animals*—but this smell was far wilder, more exciting. And there was also something weirdly warm despite the brutal cold. A musk like the Others made, something active and nervous, yet different from anything Dren had ever smelled before. She wanted to find its source and bury her face in it. Her stomach began to growl.

"Come on, it's OK…"

But the Others were not pointing her toward the smells. Instead, they were moving toward another box. This one loomed much bigger than any of Dren's other places, and its huge, sloping roof dripped with ominous shadows. It emitted a stench so dense she could almost see it: a musty, decaying, abandoned smell. Inert and unclean. It smelled like something dead. Dren's system fired off powerful flight signals as the Others marched her toward this deathly place—even though there came a thickening smell of fear from the Female. Her heavy coat and furry hat couldn't hide it; her fear sang out like a siren, shouting at Dren that they were going somewhere very definitely Bad. Why was this happening? She struggled against her swaddling, but they clung on tighter. Was she being punished? Dren tried to think of what she might have done to deserve this.

"Hey, what is it? Come on, it's just a barn!"

The Male was speaking gently, as if to cover the alarm

signals coming from the Female. She cooed at Dren reassuringly, but Dren's sensitive ears caught the quiver in her voice. Dren tried to step backward, the cold beginning to numb her feet to the sharp little things stabbing up through the blanket of white and sticking in her skin, but the Others kept pushing her forward. The exaggerated sweetness in their voices made her even more afraid. Her fear began to turn to anger. She dug her toes into the prickly ground, refusing to budge, and they tightened their grip—but as they did so, she made an exciting discovery. The blanket they had wrapped her in was so smooth that it was sort of *slippery*. The fabric slid along her skin like liquid. It gave Dren a great idea.

She ducked.

The sleeping bag suddenly deflated in Clive and Elsa's arms. Before they knew what had happened, they heard Dren scampering off into the primordial forest encircling the farm. An unearthly howl of freedom echoed behind the alien footprints that seemed to spontaneously appear in the snow and vanish into the brambles between the trees.

"Dren!"

They wasted no time retrieving flashlights from the van and following Dren's tracks into the woods. They called out for the fugitive, imploring her to return, and listened in between for the slightest noise. The forest creaked and groaned like a settling house, and the occasional sound of its nocturnal residents was indistinguishable from that of their stealthy quarry.

"Everything's fine, everything's under control, huh? Is it really under control now?"

Elsa was amazed that Clive found the energy to snipe at her even now. Hours ago, he had damned her for failing to bring up the farm, and now he damned her doubly for moving them all out there. It seemed like there wasn't much she could do right lately, and this place had resurrected the ancient feeling of always being wrong, always an inconvenience, always a disappointment. She felt herself regressing back to a state of juvenile victimhood and fought to cling to the present. She needed to tune Clive out, to train her senses on Dren's trail. Shadows danced before her eyes, blending together and defying definition.

"I really need you to calm down. We just need to focus."

"Unbelievable! This is the disaster everyone warns about: A new species, set loose in the world—"

"Don't worry, alright? She's not going to leave us."

"She just did!"

"We're gonna find her. She's not going to go far."

Elsa resented having to manage Clive's hysteria when this was much harder for her than it was for him. The return to her mother's home was already gnawing at her nerves, and now there was the compounding fear of losing…what? Who? Elsa caught herself thinking something that would make Clive *really* mad if he could read her mind. Whatever else Dren was to her, she was definitely Elsa's only friend at this point. Now Elsa was in danger of losing that hard-won connection, in addition to her future, her partner, and her sanity.

A happy gurgle emanated from a nearby thicket. Elsa and Clive froze in their tracks.

"Where is she?" Clive hissed.

They held their breath, straining their ears until another cheerful chirrup drew them in the right direction. They crept across the frozen earth, following the familiar coos and clicks until the tangled undergrowth gave way to a small clearing. There they spotted a pajama-clad figure with moonlight reflecting off her bald pate.

"Dren? Dren, honey?"

Mercifully, she didn't bolt at the sound of their approach. She was fussing over something in her lap, something that had her full attention.

"I think she's hurt," Clive whispered, but Elsa sensed something else in her posture. She didn't seem hurt. She seemed excited.

When the creature turned around, Elsa saw something that she was unable to process. Dren's face had changed shape—or had it just changed color? Beneath her sparkling, innocent eyes was a smear of something thick and curdled, and patched all over with hair. A dark, slick substance hung in ropes from her jaws. Elsa's heart leapt into her throat. *Was* she hurt? Was she sick? Was this some grotesque, new quirk of her pubescence? But as Dren turned fully toward their flashlights, they saw it: Her fists were full of not only hair, but *hare*. The unfortunate beast was half in Dren's hands, half in her teeth, and she twittered contentedly as a length of torn intestine flopped out of her maw. She could not have been more pleased with herself.

"Oh, Dren," Elsa sighed, resisting the urge to collapse as their recovered captive plunged in for another satisfying bite.

The lights of the pasteurization barn sprang to life as Elsa slammed the master switch into the On position, and Clive let out a cheer. With the generator going, the place wasn't nearly as gloomy as it looked from the outside. Actually, it had been sealed off so successfully that it hadn't taken them much time to make it basically livable. There was still a ubiquitous film of dust all around, and you wouldn't want to eat off the floor, but they could have done a lot worse for a new lab, all things considered. The peaked ceiling reached high over their heads, and there was plenty of room for Dren to stretch her legs. She would even be able to enjoy the sun when it came through the skylights and helped their space heaters fend off the cold. For now, she crouched in the hay loft overlooking the sprawling workspace, sulking.

Elsa's mother died as she had lived, leaving everything in perfect order, perhaps assuming that her prodigal daughter would return to do the lifelong penance of running the place. When the death notice came, Elsa made sure to have as little to do with her mother's last things as possible. Having no other relations (none that she knew how to reach, anyway), Elsa gave whatever cash was left to the farm's skeleton staff to close everything down. Even the notion of selling the place was too involved for her, required too much acknowledgment. Whatever money she could have made from it would have been tainted by guilt and obligation. It was preferable to simply turn her back and walk away.

"It's almost full!" Clive called from the worn wooden lip of the pasteurization vat. Ever the gear head, learning a new process had proven to be a pleasant distraction for Clive. With a little instruction from Elsa, he managed to draw water from the irrigation system into the vat's double-walled steel jacket, which heated the main basin. The basin itself had been scrubbed clean and was now, as Clive proudly noted, nearly at capacity. The whole thing was about the circumference of a standard, suburban above-ground pool. He snickered at the thought of Dren, Elsa and himself stomping around in circles to make a whirlpool, like he and Gavin had done as kids, though it was too deep for even him to stand in with his head above water.

Dren's amphibious nature remained mysterious to Clive and Elsa. She hadn't had another episode like the one that led to the discovery of her gills, but they didn't know what had caused the attack, or why submersion had resolved it. At NERD, they couldn't observe her in a proper marine environment, which made of the whole topic a frustrating and somewhat threatening blank. One special advantage of the barn was the vat; if they kept it full and warm, then Dren could self-regulate her aquatic activity. At the very least, swimming might keep her amused.

For now, Dren wasn't interested in amusement, or in anything to do with Clive or Elsa. She had been pouting since they muscled her into the barn, not letting them forget that they had spoiled her supper. Elsa had padlocked the door to keep the creature from going for more takeout, which she seemed to notice with annoyance; Elsa would have to be very mindful of the key she hung from a chain around her neck. With the premises secured, she turned toward the loft.

"Dren, you must never, ever run off on me like that again. Do you understand?"

The hybrid hunched her shoulders up around her ears, firmly facing the wall. Her tail twitched like a cat's: *Don't come near.*

"Do you understand me? Dren, look at me. That was *bad.* Bad Dren!"

Elsa felt utterly bizarre. Something had to be said, and she was the only one who would say it, but it was disturbing to hear this punishing voice come out of her mouth. She was a fighter, to be sure, but she fought for herself. She had fought for loans, for grants, for contracts, for terms and conditions. For credit. For control. But now, as she disciplined Dren, this commanding voice was nother own. She knew whose it was, recognized its brutal authority with an inward shiver. The barn was getting to her. The old aromas of motor oil and decaying hay sent a steady stream of cortisol coursing through her veins.

With a shy little click, Dren glanced over her shoulder. Elsa could see in the hybrid's wounded eyes that she had more than gotten her point across, and she was stung by a pang of guilt. This was her first real fight with the grown-up Dren, the one who had thoughts and feelings, not just animal moods and cravings. The hybrid's eyes conveyed injury, embarrassment, confusion. Elsa tried again.

"Look, I'm sorry sweetie," she attempted, lowering her voice. "I'm not angry with you. I was just...I was really worried!"

Dren looked away again, whining softly. Elsa realized she had no idea how to talk to her now. When she was little, it wasn't so hard. You talked to a child and a pet in more or less the same exaggerated manner, known as "parentese" to linguists. Elsa had learned that this bubbly affect grabbed the attention of babies and spurred their conversational development; she was relieved when she read that this style of speaking was a matter of instinct for adults, something automatic, and not a sign that she was becoming a sap. But all of a sudden, Dren had become a teenager. They had no idea what her ultimate lifespan would be, nor, since she neither spoke nor wrote, what her mental and emotional processes were really like. Treating her like a young adult was tempting, but was it appropriate?

"Well, it ain't the W., but it's got a kind of rustic charm," Clive quipped as he appeared at Elsa's side with an armful of clean bedding. His unstoppable nesting drive was in full throttle; if he had his way, the place would be wallpapered in slick C-prints of street photography and populated by limited edition vinyl kaiju by the end of the week.

"You OK, Dren?" he called up casually. Nothing. "I got a little blanket for you!"

Faster than the eye could see, Dren whirled around and flung herself toward them with a hair-raising roar. No sooner had she hit the ground than her powerful legs propelled her into the air several feet over their heads before she cannonballed into the vat and sank to the bottom.

After a stunned beat, delayed panic washed over Elsa, as if she'd narrowly missed being hit by a bus. *Jesus Christ, she's so strong now. When did that happen?* Dren was powerful even when she was little, but as she'd grown up and learned to behave herself, Clive and Elsa had fewer opportunities to find out how threatening she might have become. They had assumed too much about their creation from her conception, about how to keep her safe, and also whether they would be safe from her.

As the shock wore off, Elsa began to feel oddly insulted. She had tried to level with the Dren, to show her sympathy and concern; to give the halfling something better than what Elsa had grown up with. But her olive branch had been rejected, and now she was all wet. Dren couldn't slam the door to her room like a normal kid, but she found an even better option at the bottom of the vat.

"Maybe we should move her into the house," Elsa stammered.

"Now way, come on! Someone's gonna see her in there." Clive was right. The nearest neighbors were miles away, but if one of them happened to notice a ruckus in the abandoned Kast place, they might be tempted to investigate. "This is fine. She needs a place to be in water. She's just upset! Everything's new."

Clive's newfound compassion was chafing. Somehow, when he was mad at Dren, it was only rational, but when Elsa had a problem with her, then it was Elsa herself who was the problem. She had been the only one to make the slightest effort with Dren so far, and now Clive was doing his best to make her feel like she was being uncool. She felt the urge to fight rise from her gut and swallowed it as he tousled her hair and rubbed her shoulders. Exhaustion was wearing away her resistance.

"Come on, let's move in. It's late, OK?" Clive rubbed his hands together and breathed into them, signaling his desire for a nice warm bed.

Lets move in. Into the place she had done everything in her power to leave behind. A twinge of panic sent her flying backward in time and space. In another world, Elsa let Clive talk her into leasing a bigger loft; let him put a baby in her; let him defer all her dreams so they could start a normal family and live happily ever after. If only she'd given in, if only she'd traded in her scrubs for an apron and their circulating bath for a bottle warmer. If only she had done these things, then maybe she wouldn't be here, now.

The crisp snow sounded impossibly loud under their boots as they approached the dark, silent farmhouse. The handsome two-story redbrick home with its decorative white eaves and wraparound veranda might have looked inviting in the daylight—if it were anything but Elsa's childhood home. She would have preferred a bona fide haunted house to this house that so haunted her. She had stopped several yards from the entrance. Clive watched her patiently.

"You OK?"

"Yeah, of course. It's just a house."

And yet it took all her willpower to take the next step. She was nagged by the feeling that she was committing a crime, sneaking back inside under cover of night after meeting a boy at the end of the old access road. She automatically braced herself for punishment, even though her jailer was long gone. She allowed Clive to lead her up to the front steps, where the beam of his flashlight picked out the solid oak door.

It had been left unlocked.

Elsa held her breath as they stepped over the threshold. The floorboards groaned under their feet as if waking from a long slumber. Dust had fallen over the pale sheets covering her mother's Shaker furniture. The damp had stained the creamy wallpaper, and spiders wove shrouds for the built-in hutches and hearth. The home could once have been considered tasteful, though Elsa's mother would have condemned any discussion of aesthetics. Elsa still felt the weight of her authority everywhere. It was as if after her earthly death, the woman's soul had infused itself into the house's timbers, and it had become her body. Within its walls, Elsa had the old sense of being a mere extension of her mother. Despite the years this tomb stood empty, a smell met her nose that she could not have described to another person, but that put her on high alert.

Their footfalls echoed in Elsa's ears as they climbed the stairs, and she fought the instinct to be neither seen nor heard as they approached her childhood bedroom. The door swung open with a faint whine, and she had the sensation that the room itself shrank with embarrassment under the beams of their flashlights. This was a different world from that of the stately first floor chambers. Wire hangers, some bent and twisted out of shape, hung from metal coat hooks screwed directly into the wall.

The peeling white wallpaper held little trace of its original pattern, and it blended almost seamlessly with the threadbare curtains hanging across the single narrow window, the dowdy slipcover on a tiny chair, and the institutional sheet carelessly thrown over a twin mattress lying on the floor. An ancient toy chest in the corner was empty, Elsa knew, because it had always been empty—except when she was inside of it. An old steel pot sat ominously in the middle of the room, and everything was covered in detritus from the crumbling ceiling.

"This was your room?" Clive asked incredulously.

"Mmhm."

"I thought you said your mom left it just the way it was."

Elsa might have found Clive's disturbance satisfying in some way, but that he should have known by now. Should have begun to guess where she came from, why she didn't speak about the farm. She glanced at him sharply as she headed for the master bedroom.

"She did."

7

"Nice of you to show up!"

Barlow was using his Boss Voice, a new affectation that made him less likable than ever before.

"Traffic," Clive grunted.

The project manager's newfound haughtiness stuck out in the depressive atmosphere of the renovated NERD clinic. Gone was the air of comradery, the boomboxes bumping adrenalizing mixes, and colorful novelties Clive hid here and there to pep up the place. That void had been filled by an embarrassment of new gear, new supplies, new everything, forming a claustrophobic labyrinth that forced people to squeeze past one another on the way to their obscure destinations.

A few clinicians glanced up at Clive and Elsa but did not greet them. The place was full of strangers now, and people who had become like strangers. Some were Barlow's recruits, the kinds of humorless drones with whom he was most at home. Others were colleagues the couple once counted as being like family, who now regarded them with suspicion. The demise of Fred and Ginger had done its damage, and the surrender to Barlow salted the wound. Clive and Elsa shriveled with guilt. They had just left a sulking, unpredictable Dren all alone at the farm for the first time, miles away, and here at the clinic they were faced with even more people they'd abandoned. It was as if they had returned to an orphanage to collect children who no longer recognized them.

Barlow thrust a pair of lab coats into their hands with a cold, tight grin.

"You will observe protocol. It's the only way we're gonna beat this thing," he declared with theatrical authority as they shrugged on their uniforms. "Thank you. Shall we get to work?"

Dren had been alone before, but never like this. She had always been aware of life going on around her. She could sense thrumming machines somewhere, and Others creeping around outside the walls of her rooms. Now everything was different. She knew for certain that there was not a single Other around. No one to catch her or scare her or command her. No one to hide from. For the very first time, she was all on her own.

Dren was not lonely. She was exhilarated. She remembered how the World yawned open all around her when they arrived at the new place, and she knew that it was still out there. She could smell the breeze slipping in through the slats of her new home, carrying the promise of Plants and Animals, and she could hear it rustle the great dark spires where she had caught her first meal all by herself. Water dripped down mysteriously from the ceiling, making musical sounds as it fell around her. There was a little machine here that glowed red inside and radiated an inviting warmth (she had learned the hard way not to touch it), and it made a *hissss* when the droplets hit it. Even the surfaces here were new to her; nothing was as slick and solid as in the places she once knew, but this place was full of soft, uneven textures, with winding lines and circles within circles. Big blocky stacks of dry Plant matter in the corners gave off a scent of decay that was strangely comforting once you got used to it. It was beautiful here—and best of all, she even had her own room! Dren's bed was set up by a stall that the Others had cleaned out and filled with blankets and toys. It didn't have a door, but still, Dren could go in there when she was feeling private.

Now, with the Others gone, the whole place was private. A bright light poured through the windows in the roof, and Dren drifted from one warm shaft to another. She stuck out her long, pointed tongue and caught droplets of water as they fell from the ceiling. Even water was different here! It had new flavors that seemed to be full of information. She loved the icy sensation of it sliding down her gullet. As she paced around with her mouth open, she sang. This, too, was a new experience. In the before places, she was always being told to *be quiet*. In here, all by herself, she could open up. She let out a long, undulating tone that bounced back to her from the walls of the great big box. It was a little bit like the chattering sounds the Others made, but Dren thought her sound was much prettier.

Of course, she still wished she could make the sounds the Others made. She had been trying, secretly, quietly. In the other places, she was surrounded by symbols, and the Female taught her how the symbols and things were connected by sounds. Dren had learned quite a lot of sounds—her own name, the names of places she had to go, and things she had to do—but only a few of the symbols that went with them. The Male didn't seem to like these lessons, so the Female kept them short. But Dren was a very curious creature. She listened closely to the sounds the Others made, and if she tried hard, she could connect their sounds to their actions. If she figured out one thing—like the sound and symbols for *Dren*—she could use that to figure out more things, like *Dinner*, and *Don't*. Dren could tell the Others thought she wasn't as smart as them, but they were wrong. She could figure out a lot of things from knowing just a little. She was much, much smarter than they thought.

Understanding a sound was different from making the sound, though. Dren tried and tried, but she just couldn't chatter like the Others. She could make many sounds that they could not, which sometimes made her feel better than them, but they went on bossing her around, which made her feel worse. Dren's sense of better-than and worse-than was a recent development. Good and bad seemed to have to do with needs, where better and worse was about wants. Dren was forced to hide so often that it began to feel as if she wasn't wanted. The Female used to make her feel wanted, but lately she was acting more like the Males: scared and mad. Dren worried about this, but she didn't know what to do.

Anyway, Dren didn't feel like worrying now. She wanted to keep her private party going. She climbed up to the hayloft and tiptoed over scattered stuffed animals to a table where the Female had left the little box for Dren. All the strange enchantments of the big new place still couldn't compete with the treasures inside this box, the very best of which was the mirror. This was truly amazing. Dren had seen her own reflection in some of the slick surfaces of the other places, but it was always dark and soft, like a shadow. This surface showed her what she really looked like for the very first time. And she never grew tired of looking, even if it sometimes made her feel uneasy.

Dren opened the box and stared into the glass. At first, she loved to look at herself, to see all the different things her face could do. The Female was so delighted by her antics that it made Dren feel good about herself, like she must be nice to look at. But then, inevitably, the mirror taught her to compare herself with the Others. She looked rather like them—their eyes, noses, mouths, and ears were all in the same place (sort of), and they had the same limbs (well, mostly)—but they never seemed to change, while Dren was changing all the time. She would squint into the mirror for long stretches, wondering what these changes meant, until she was pried away to do some trick or take some test. The only thing that seemed to change about the Others was their hair.

Dren pulled the shiny golden crown out of the box and put it on her head. The little ends poked into her bare scalp, but she didn't mind. The crown was set with glittering bits of creamy white and transparent blue that sparkled as she turned her head, making her mirror image even more exciting. Rummaging around some more, she found a metal toy with something inside it that made a loud rattling sound when she shook it. It was fun to hear it echo in this new place, but something about it perplexed her; she could make a rattle like that too, inside herself, but she didn't usually do it for fun. Replacing the noisemaker, she retrieved an object that truly mystified her: a piece of paper that held a real-life image. It showed two Females, a big one and a little one, both with long yellow hair. The image reminded Dren of her Female, and Dren tried to make her speak about it, but the Female made it very clear that she never would.

Digging deeper, Dren found something else that reminded her of the Female: the doll with the gold hair. It seemed that the Others liked to collect things that resembled themselves. Dren held the doll next to her own face in the mirror and studied the differences. The body looked kind of like hers, but... She ran her fingers through the long, shiny hair. Even the Male had long hair; maybe not AS long, but it was something that he and the Female enjoyed. They could arrange it in different ways, and they liked to touch each other's hair, too. Dren noticed an unpleasant feeling growing inside her. Something in her chest felt heavy, and her cheeks grew hot. She didn't quite understand it, but she didn't like it. Before it got any worse, she yanked the crown off her head and stuffed everything back in the box—when she heard a *sound*.

Dren was not alone. Some*thing* was making a noise that she had never heard before: part way between a purr and a yowl. Then she smelled it! She had been so distracted by the box that she missed this warm, wafting aroma, like she had smelled outside the night before. A soft, wet smacking sound met her ears. Dren growled involuntarily, and so did her stomach. As quiet as could be, she leaned over the edge of the loft and spotted it.

A small, fluffy white animal sat on the table below, lapping at the food containers that the Others had forgotten to put away. It was a similar size to Dren's dinner from the night before, but a different shape, with short pointy ears, black spots, and a long tail like Dren had. It was the first time she had seen a living thing with this same part. She figured she had better be careful. Oh so slowly, she got down on her belly and slid as far to the edge of the loft as she could. She reached down, down, down… and snatched the critter off the table. It let out a helpless yowl and lashed out with its claws, but Dren held it tight and ran as fast as she could to her stall at the end of the barn.

She held the animal up to the light to get a better look at its twitching tail, its little pink paw pads, its soft belly. She had toys that looked very much like this. She never knew there were live ones. Little by little, it stopped resisting her. It studied her, its whiskers tickling her face as it touched its cold, wet nose to hers. Dren pressed it to her breast and rubbed her cheek against its warm fur, and it began to make a low, rumbling purr. It liked to be held tight like this, and so did Dren, when she felt afraid. They sat together for a long time listening to the water drip down from the roof and smelling all the smells that drifted in through the walls.

"THERE ARE 26 LETTERS, THERE ARE 26 LETTERS, THERE ARE 26 LETTERS IN THE AL-PHA-BET!"

The jangly children's tape blaring out of the boombox was beginning to drive Elsa a little bonkers, but she told herself that it was good for Dren's cognitive development. Elsa didn't have much time to teach her lately. After slaving away on Phase 2 all day under Barlow's watchful eye, she barely had the energy left to feed their little family, let alone read and write with their sulky child. In truth, she was losing track of what phase they were supposed to be in with Dren. What were they supposed to be doing with her now, besides basic maintenance? Between the roar of the juicer mixing up the creature's gloppy dinner, the buffoonish bellowing from the boombox, and the scream of the power drill Clive was using to install security cameras, Elsa had a hard time focusing on anything.

She poured the green slurry into a mixing bowl, dropped a spoon into it, and sat down next to Dren. Elsa pushed the bowl toward the creature, displacing the Scrabble tiles she had been playing with. She glanced up irritably and shoved the bowl back at Elsa, spreading the tiles out again. Elsa took a deep breath.

"Please honey, not today. Eat your dinner, OK?"

"She doesn't like that stuff," Clive grunted. "Maybe she wants meat!"

"She doesn't eat meat," Elsa shot back.

"I'm sorry, is rabbit considered a vegetable?" he scoffed.

"That was an accident!"

Since when did he become the expert? Clive had barely fed Dren since her baster days, yet now he was judging Elsa's homemaking skills from the top of a ladder, far from the battlefield of the dinner table. Meanwhile, Elsa was bending over backwards to make sure their creation got some form of decent nutrition. She was aging rapidly, and they might have a little old lady on their hands any week now. She needed vitamins and minerals, not high fructose corn syrup.

Elsa studied the young adult sitting across the table. Dren's wardrobe consisted chiefly of nightgowns, considering her inhuman lower tract. The current selection was a baggy flannel number with lacy pink frills. It didn't suit her. Dren was turning into a woman already. She was taller than Elsa, but slender like her, with similarly refined features. Her vertical seam was nearly invisible now, and despite her wide-set eyes with their star-shaped pupils, one could call her lovely. If anything, the frumpy nightgown threw into stark relief her maturity and grace. *We should be sending her off to college about now,* Elsa caught herself thinking.

"Come on, honey," she said, sliding the mixing bowl back under Dren's nose. "I know you're hungry. Eat your din—"

Dren swiftly moved the bowl out of Elsa's grasp and returned to the tiles with increased urgency. Elsa struggled to keep the anger out of her voice.

"What is it? What's the matter?"

Dren rapidly arranged tiles in a deliberate sequence.

T E D I

"What? *Tedi—*"

Elsa watched in amazement as Dren completed her thought. After lining up three more tiles, the creature fixed Elsa with a pleading stare. Flabbergasted, Elsa called out to Clive.

"She spelled TEDIOUS!"

Clive squinted down at them in confusion and descended the ladder.

"Where would she get a word like that?"

"I don't know. She's telling us she's bored!"

Elsa's annoyance dissipated. She saw the pout pulling at the corners of Dren's mouth and recognized it as one she used to wear all the time, here on the farm. The sad, anxious look of someone who is being held back, tamped down, unrecognized. The momentary thrill of Dren spelling an SAT word was all but forgotten in the face of Elsa's overpowering guilt.

"She's been stuck here for a week. Do you want to play a game or something, sweetie?"

Dren created a new sequence of tiles, tapping them with her pearl grey nails. She looked back at Elsa and squeaked tragically. Clive looked on, slack-jawed. This time, she hadn't just spelled a word. She made an anagram.

OUTSIDE

"Holy shit, how did you…"

Dren slammed her palms down on the table, jumbling the tiles. Her chest heaved with frustration. She wasn't trying to impress them. She didn't want treats. She was desperately trying to communicate. Elsa took a breath and mustered up her most maternal attitude.

"Oh Dren, I know," Elsa said, dripping with sincerity. "I'm sorry, but you can't go outside. You know, you just ca—"

Dren exploded. She roared to her feet, flipping the table, and tore through the makeshift kitchen, ravaging their food stores. Pots and pans flew over her shoulders like bombs, keeping the humans at bay.

"No, Dren, stop it!" Elsa cried impotently as Clive stepped up to bat, making a suppressive gesture with his outstretched palms.

"Hey, cut it out!" He said in what he hoped was a measured tone, moving in on the enraged creature. "Dren, take it easy—"

She turned on him and he froze in terror. Holding his gaze defiantly, she sent a set of utility shelves crashing to the floor, spraying broken glass around his feet. He was too stunned to react. Elsa was not.

"You know what, that's it!" she shouted, twisting Dren's elbow and digging her fingers into the back of her neck. "You come over here right now and sit down! SIT DOWN!"

Dren was subdued instantly. Curling her head into her chest and throwing her hands up defensively, she yelped as Elsa forced her back into her chair.

"Hey, hey, Elsa! Cool it!" Clive said, inserting himself between the two combatants. He grasped Elsa firmly by the shoulders and backed her away from the war zone. "Come on."

"You saw what she did! Did you not see what she did? *Fuck!*"

"I did! Stop, it's OK," Clive murmured, creating even more distance from Dren. "It's OK, it's done."

Flushed and wild-eyed, Elsa choked back tears of frustration. "She's just getting so hard to control, I can't—"

An explosion of glass rained down on them from above, and they looked up just in time to see Dren disappearing through a skylight.

"Dren, STOP!" Elsa cried over the creature's tortured wail as she vanished from sight.

Clive and Elsa raced outside and hustled up a warped wooden ladder to the roof. It flexed under their weight as an icy north wind threatened to send them back down to the earth. Clive took Elsa's hand and hoisted her up the slope of the gable roof under the rapidly blackening sky. Their boots slipped and slid over the dusting of snow on the ancient shingles.

"Dren, come back here!"

"Come on, sweetie, come back inside!"

Dren tiptoed along the roof's peak, clasping her hands at her breast as the wind whipped her nightgown around her hips. She gazed up at the heavy clouds ringed with silver by the moon behind them. So enamored was she by this sight that she nearly stepped off the roof into thin air.

"Dren, we're not angry!" Clive called out in desperation.

The couple moved as one over the treacherous snow toward the escapee. Suddenly Elsa's feet slid out from under her, and Clive barely caught her in time to drag her up to the turret-like cupola. As they clung to its vents for dear life, Elsa heard her mother's voice come tearing out of her throat.

"Dren, GET BACK HERE THIS INSTANT!"

At last, Dren spun around. Elsa's face was the last thing she saw as the shingles splintered under her feet, and she tipped backward into the void. The two helpless humans watched as the creature's arms pinwheeled in space. Her eyes widened with heartbreaking surprise as her toes left the roof. She opened her mouth to scream.

And then, Dren changed.

Her frightened scream transformed into a primal roar as a freakish tearing sound was heard. Her nightgown was shredded by two sets of wings that blew open like sails from her forearms and triceps. They caught the wind perfectly, pulling her back to the safety of the roof. Crisscrossing black veins shot through the billowing membranes in a stained-glass effect, like the wings of a dragonfly.

No sooner had Dren regained her footing, than she unleashed another awful shriek and snapped forward at the waist. Two fan-like protrusions erupted from between her shoulder blades. These stood straight up like saw blades, scaffolded by sharp, stiff spines.

For a moment she froze there, displaying herself to the two inferior beings cowering against the cupola. A threat display, Elsa thought fearfully. The new flaps flowed around Dren like the fins of an enormous betta fish. Then she spun around, facing the treetops. She was preparing for takeoff.

By some miracle, Clive broke through his paralysis and began to inch toward her, reaching out with open arms.

"Dren! Dren don't," he begged, and lowered his voice. Sympathy. Humility. Honesty. "We need you!"

The creature hesitated. Gaining confidence, Clive continued to advance.

"Dren...we love you."

Her body stiffened as if in shock. The wind carried a soft whine to their ears as her body spasmed. With a series of jerky movements and a visceral cracking sound, her wings slid slowly back into the long, clean fissures in her flesh. She shuddered as they finally disappeared, before spinning around and flinging herself into Clive's embrace.

"Come here," he whispered as he gathered her to him. She

surrendered completely. Her eyes turned heavenward in an expression of profound catharsis.

Elsa watched from the cupola with a mix of emotions that twisted her stomach in a knot. Some of what she felt was simple shock. The crisis had left her weak in the knees, and she hadn't wrapped her mind around Dren's latest evolution. She could deal with that later; there would be time to examine her in the light once they were all safe and warm inside the barn. Something else was bothering Elsa, something that felt more urgent. Where had Clive suddenly found all this feeling?

Clive, who recoiled from baby Dren, could hardly bring himself to touch her or feed her. Who looked at Elsa with naked disgust when she cuddled the needy creature, dressed her warmly, bought her toys, and gave her a name. Clive, who for so long would only call her *It*. For whose sake Elsa had wrestled with her unscientific feelings of affection for Dren, hiding their true depth from his judgment. Clive, who stood back and sneered as Elsa tried hard to be firm and fair with their moody, adolescent ward. Clive, who had begged to put Dren down like a dog before she grew up healthy and strong. And beautiful.

He remained there at the edge of nothing as Dren wound herself around him like a vine. Her grateful purring could be heard over the wind. He had saved her life, accepted her at long last, and yet what Elsa felt was not relief.

She had been betrayed.

8

William Barlow squinted at the Gantt charts that tracked his team's progress on Phase 2. This was taking far longer than it should. He knew he wouldn't be able to fend off Joan Charot much longer, and he shuddered at the thought of her laser beam gaze reducing him to ash. He sighed and glanced at his watch, drumming his fingers on the counter irritably. What the hell was going on with the dream team? They should be driving this project, not holding it back. He shoved his chair back from the makeshift office he'd set up at amid stores of test tubes, flasks, and Petri dishes, nearly knocking into a pair of clinicians working right behind him. He needed to have a little talk with NERD's prodigal parents.

He found Clive and Gavin huddled together over a rotary evaporator that slowly turned a flask full of blue fluid in a heated bath. Clive did not look up from his clipboard as Barlow arrived. Just as he suspected, someone was conspicuously absent.

"Elsa not here yet?"

"Not feeling well," Clive muttered without looking up from his clipboard.

"You gotta be kidding me," Barlow groaned. He stood there

expectantly, as if Elsa would squeeze out from between the brothers if he applied enough pressure.

Clive turned to face him. The harsh fluorescent light exposed the purple rings under his bloodshot eyes and the day's growth of stubble dotting his pale skin.

"People get sick. It happens."

"A lot of people would just suck it up. You know, rise to the occasion?" Barlow sneered, standing his ground. Although Clive had already turned his back, he added spitefully, "You guys are not some special case. Not anymore."

With that, the senior project manager spun on his heels and marched back to his makeshift office. Had he waited a moment longer to see the impact of this display of power, he'd have heard Clive grumble over the hissing and chiming machinery: *"Fucking idiot."*

Dren sat on a stool before an antique vanity by the pasteurization vat. Elsa and Clive had moved so much furniture in from the house that the barn was beginning to look like an estate sale. Wingback chairs, ornately carved end tables, a solid oak credenza, an ancient steamer trunk, and other well-preserved furnishings broke up the space into little pseudo-rooms. This achieved a reasonable approximation of coziness.

After last night's unpleasant episode, Elsa had decided to take a different tack with Dren. The creature's rebellious phase was in full swing, and she no longer took kindly to cuddling, coddling, or whatever firm-but-fair theatrics Elsa deployed to keep her in line. Or maybe it was all Elsa's fault; maybe she just wasn't cut out for motherhood. No surprises there. She hadn't had a particularly good role model, and though she still couldn't bring herself to say it to Clive's face, she had never been able to picture herself playing the part.

In the early days of their experiment, when Dren needed a

lot of care, Elsa was shocked by the strength of feeling that the little critter brought out in her. She was so small and vulnerable, and so receptive to affection and protection; next to Clive, Elsa must have seemed extremely maternal. But now, Dren's newfound independent streak was changing everything. She didn't understand or, more likely, didn't care that the discipline Elsa doled out was for her own safety. Didn't want to hang around the pseudo-house all day with her de facto parents. Didn't want to eat her vegetables. And it certainly didn't help that Clive was always lurking in the background, laughing at Elsa's attempts to raise a healthy hybrid, carping about her culinary skills, rolling his eyes at her version of homeschooling. He relished the role of the fun uncle while Elsa transformed into a stern schoolmarm.

Whatever Clive and Dren thought of her, Elsa wasn't enjoying this. She constantly wondered when things would go back to the way they were. She and Dren used to be buddies, bonding over what a bad dad Clive turned out to be. Now she found herself on the wrong end of the good cop-bad cop equation. Or maybe it was more like cloth mother-wire mother.

In any case, Dren had decided she didn't want to be mothered anymore. Not by Elsa, anyway. Fine. She could work with that. Today she was taking a more sororal approach. Elsa was an only child, but she had sometimes imagined what it would be like to have a sister. What is it like to have someone like Gavin in your life, who had been there for everything that ever happened to you, who knew exactly why you turned out the way you did? It boggled the mind. Elsa not only lacked sisters, but she'd never had any female friends.

When she was younger, getting along better with boys felt like a badge of honor. They were impressed by her ruggedness and fierce intelligence, which stood in stark contrast to her petiteness and pretty face. If she refused to become their girlfriend, they'd settle for the thrill of her beating them at games, sports, science trivia, and whatever else they came up with to while away their dull, rural childhood. Girls, on the other hand, usually saw Elsa's strength and smarts as a bad thing. They called her names she'd never heard, and she got in trouble for asking her mother what they meant. Girls were vain and petty and unserious, Elsa told herself, while she privately struggled with the pageantry of teenage femininity. She had to learn everything on her own.

Dren held very still while Elsa dusted blush onto her cheeks. She had already applied an eye-catching dash of lipstick, and ringed her eyes with a smoky liner before drawing out her surprisingly long lashes with mascara. She's got excellent bone structure, Elsa thought as she admired her handiwork.

"My mother wouldn't let me wear makeup. She said that it debased women," Elsa confided as she put the final brush-strokes on her living canvas. Then she reflected, with a sly smirk, "But who doesn't want to be debased every once in a while?"

Dren didn't take her meaning, and it struck Elsa as ironic that she'd got the creature all dolled up with no place to go. That didn't matter much, though; girls work on their looks as much to impress themselves as they do to get attention from boys. It was a matter of self-esteem. It was part of one's identity.

"Look!" Elsa said, spinning Dren toward the vanity. "See how pretty you've become?"

When Dren saw the mirror, her brow furrowed. She squinted at her reflection with a confused squeak, leaning toward the glass to inspect herself more closely. Elsa had skill-fully exaggerated the exotic contours of her face, and with her new smoldering eye and scarlet pout, Dren looked downright sultry. To complete her makeover, Elsa had donated a grownup sundress with a generous neckline that showed off Dren's deli-cate collarbones and shoulder blades. A heart-shaped gold locket hung from a fine chain around her slender neck, and Elsa had briefly considered piercing her ears, before thinking better of it. That Ambystoma gene would probably close them right back up, anyway.

"You're gonna have to learn to be a grownup," Elsa grinned as her creation pondered the mirror ambivalently. She gave Dren's shoulders an encouraging squeeze. "I remember how I felt at your age. It's an exciting time. I never thought it—"

She cut herself off. What was she even going to say? She never thought she'd be doing this with her own little girl. She had to be careful not to say such things, especially around Clive. Dren was watching her with concern.

"Maybe we could use some more eyeliner, hm?" Elsa stammered, forcing a smile. "Let's try some more eyeliner."

Where did that stupid pencil go? She scanned the cosmetics scattered on the vanity and the floor below. She opened one of its drawers in case she'd unconsciously put it where it belonged and was surprised by what she found instead. Dren abruptly turned away as Elsa pulled out a stack of rumpled papers.

"What are these?"

On each sheet was a colored pencil drawing of a man's face. He had green eyes, a friendly smile, and floppy brown hair. The drawings were crude, but they were remarkably well-proportioned—the work of a child who will become the best artist in her class. The features were instantly recognizable as Clive's.

"Did you do these?"

She knew that there were colored pencils among the childhood treasures she'd given Dren, but she hadn't given them much thought, even though there was plenty of paper around. Her instinct had been to cultivate Dren's intellect, to test her IQ; it hadn't occurred to Elsa that she might enjoy art-making. It just wasn't her area. She wondered where the impulse came from, and quickly realized that it wasn't a mystery. All children draw, they only stop when their peers start to sort out who is "good" at it from who is "bad", and it becomes a matter of competition. Elsa hadn't drawn anything but schematics since she was a little girl.

"These are really good!" she declared as she paged through the stack. "Are there any of me?"

Dren snatched the drawings out of her hands with a resentful snarl and raced across the barn to her stall. After a breathless beat, Elsa followed, bracing herself for another emotional scene. She cautiously peeked in to find Dren curled up in her nest of toys and blankets with a cat purring contentedly in her lap.

"Dren, what is that?" Elsa snapped.

Dren held the docile beast more tightly, and it purred louder. *Jesus Christ*, Elsa thought, *it probably belongs to somebody!*. Maybe her mother used to feed it? It was hard to imagine the woman voluntarily caring for anything but herself. In any case, Elsa couldn't have any uncontrolled intrusions. *It might have ticks, or worms, or who knows what. Just wait until she eats it, then we'll have problems we really don't need.*

"Where did you get that?" she barked. "Give it to me! Dren, you give it to me right now."

Elsa wrested the stowaway from Dren's arms and stared down at her coldly. She hardened her heart against the creature's crestfallen cries. Now this was something for which Elsa'd had a great role model. It hurt Elsa's heart to discipline baby Dren, who didn't know any better, but now she was old enough to understand the rules. She had to know that broken rules have consequences.

"Sorry, you can't keep her," Elsa said in her best *"this is for your own good voice"*, something she heard coming out of her own mouth more and more these days. At least she hadn't gone with *"this hurts you more than it hurts me,"* which her mother loved to repeat, and which was never, ever true.

"We can't take a chance, alright? It could make you sick."

She turned on her heels and headed for the exit with the mewling intruder. As Dren's mournful keening rose in volume, Elsa's blood started to simmer. That spoiled little bitch really doesn't know how good she has it. She turned back one last time, staring down her nose at the pitiful creature whose arms still reached out for her furry friend.

"You can't always get what you want," Elsa concluded with satisfaction. "That's a part of growing up, too."

Clive returned from his shift in the gene mines to a confusing scene. The barn was silent. Dren was hidden away in some dark corner, but Elsa was nowhere to be found. That wasn't right. She had supposedly played hooky to make nice with the hybrid, not to abandon her; if anything, Elsa should at least be monitoring her, charting her development, or...whatever they were supposed to be doing with her at this point. Clive scratched his head and made his way to the farmhouse.

"Elsa?"

The house, too, was eerily quiet. It was still reasonably light outside. What could she be doing? Could she have left? Clive imagined Elsa retreating to their apartment without telling him. Or maybe she'd finally snapped and taken off for parts unknown. There had been a dark cloud hovering over Elsa's head since the night before; she was stewing on something, but she wouldn't say what. He felt a twinge of panic as he climbed the stairs. He was heading for the master bedroom where they'd quartered themselves, when he noticed light coming out of Elsa's childhood bedroom.

He peeked in, and relief washed over him when he spotted her curled up on the moldering mattress. She had tossed off the patchwork quilt in her sleep. Even now, her brow was creased with worry. *At least she's not alone,* Clive thought as he noted the presence of an old barn cat sprawling comfortably beside her. What the hell had gone on here while he was at the lab? He supposed there would be time for questions later. Clive retrieved the quilt and tucked Elsa in before turning out the light and making his way to the barn.

"Dren?"

Clive followed the sounds of something like crying to one of the pine and chicken wire stalls in the far corners. There, amid a collection of rusty buckets and cleaning supplies, Dren slumped on the dusty floor.

"Shit…" He approached cautiously and crouched down next to her. "Hey, what's the matter, girl?"

When she turned to look at him, he only had more questions. Her cheeks were streaked with running mascara. Her face had been beautifully made-up, until recently anyway; now her fine features were smeared with black liner and red lipstick. She wore a sundress of Elsa's, one he remembered fondly, and jewelry, too. It looked like Dren and Elsa had been having some fun, or had tried to. She turned away again, hanging her head.

"What happened?" Clive asked softly. He reached out to stroke her cheek. "Did Elsa do that? Looks nice."

Nice? Was that the right thing to say? Did she even know what he was saying? She sure seems to understand some things, he thought, reflecting on her rooftop rescue. But she remained unpredictable. It was so hard to say how much of her was animal and how much was human. He tried patting her on the head. Is this right? Is this a normal thing to do? It didn't seem to be working. Dren's despair was impenetrable. He averted his eyes.

Clive was never too good at the sad stuff. He just didn't identify very well with angst, which was part of the reason he didn't probe too deeply when Elsa was gripped by one of her introspective moods. He was secretly grateful that she was so withholding. If she told him what was really bothering her, he might not be able to understand it. Luckily, he had other things to offer.

Putting on a casual air, he stood up and walked to the middle of the barn, surveying his surroundings.

"Well, let's lighten things up around here, eh?"

Dren watched with suspicion as he arrived at the little pine hutch that held his turntable and a selection of records. After a quick review of his archive, he slid a vinyl disc out of its sleeve and flipped it over gingerly.

"That's good, that's really good," he pretended to say to himself while attracting her attention.

He set the record on the slipmat and dropped the needle. A jaunty big band beat startled Dren out of her malaise. From the corner of his eye, Clive saw her standing at attention with a bemused look creeping over her tear-stained features. He danced with himself, snapping his fingers and turning in circles. A lilting clarinet solo carried his feet across the floor in Dren's direction.

"You like that? It's music!"

Sure enough, Dren was smiling. He hadn't seen this look on her face in a long time. *All work and no play,* he thought to himself as he bobbed along. She had Elsa breathing down her neck all the time, making her jump through hoops, and the only culture she was getting was from those maddening kiddie tapes. Dren needed some fun in her life, and that was one area where Clive definitely had Elsa beat.

"Come on, it's fun, huh? It's *music!*"

She was giggling now. Maybe at the end of the day she's just like any other teenager, Clive thought optimistically. She had sort of a riot grrrl thing going on with her baby doll frock and smudged eye makeup. He tried to remember the last time he had seen Elsa like that.

"Come on, come on, come on…" Clive whispered, as if he were calling a cat.

Fascinated, Dren settled beside him and looked him up and down. She studied his tapping toes and snapping fingers and snickered at his warbly humming.

"Come on, it's just music! You feel that?" He sucked in a deep breath and let it out with exaggerated pleasure, stretching out his arms. "It makes you feel good!"

Just as he hoped, she imitated him, letting out a gale of her strange laughter and flapping her arms excitedly. Now she was bouncing along with him.

"Feels better, yeah! Let it out!"

Dren took a spin across the floor, her skirt fluttering around her thighs. Now that she was finally letting go, there was no stopping her. She spun back to Clive, tittering manically and shaking her fists in the air.

"Good, very good! That's *dancing!*"

Clive cheered her on as she started a chaotic jig with no discernible rhythm. She was laughing up a storm. He'd never considered what kinds of moves you could do with inverted knees.

"OK! That's…kind of a dance!"

Since Elsa had canceled her own classes for the day, it was time for Clive to teach Dren something really important.

"OK, look…look at my feet! Watch my feet."

Clive pointed at the floor, and Dren's eyes followed.

"OK, ready? And ONE! Step, step…"

He started an easy-going stroll, hopping lightly from side to side as he traveled forward. Dren jumped right in. Her footwork wasn't perfect, but she easily tracked him to the middle of the floor, and then strolled backward right alongside him. Back at square one, she swayed next to him, waiting for her next cue.

"Very good. Look at you! I knew we got the dance gene in there somewhere," he laughed. *Maybe we should have called you Ginger,* he almost said—but the less Dren knew about Fred and Ginger, the better. He could explain Ginger Rogers to her later.

He turned to face her, stepping in close.

"Give me your hand."

Suspicion darkened her features again as he invited contact. He wiggled his fingers in the air over her shoulder.

"Hold my hand!"

Slowly, shyly, Dren slipped her four-fingered hand into his palm, and he clasped it gently. The sensation tickled his brain; it was like a woman's hand, with its delicate fingers and thumb, but strangely elongated. An electric charge passed between them. They had never really touched before; at least, not voluntarily or socially. Clive had helped move her in and out of boxes and assisted with examinations, but they had certainly never held hands. With this display of mutual trust, he felt the many weeks of tension between them begin to dissolve.

"That's nice. OK, hand there," he murmured, placing her other hand on his shoulder. She obeyed uncertainly. "Put it here. Very good."

She watched him intently, awaiting his next command.

"I'm gonna lead, OK?" he said as he placed his hand on her waist. Her eyes darted anxiously from his hands to his feet as he began to move to the beat again. "I'm the man, I lead. Back up, back up, one more…"

As he stepped forward, she took a nervous step back. He took another step, and she matched him again. She looked over her shoulder, afraid to fall, and he slid his hand reassuringly into the small of her back. And then he took her into a spin.

"You're a good dancer! You're *very* good. Look at you!"

Now this she loved. She relaxed into his arms and threw her head back as they whirled across the floor, her musical laughter echoing from the rafters. He felt something inside him come undone, and it felt good. What he'd said to her on the roof was true. At least, he assumed he spoke for Elsa. Sure, it had given him an icky feeling when Elsa treated the angry little tadpole like a baby. That was just inappropriate. She was still a specimen then, from an experiment that Clive felt had been forced on him. He was pissed that he'd had to remind Elsa of their scientific duties. He'd been pissed off continuously for weeks on end, and it was starting to make him sick. But then Dren started to turn into…well, into sort of a person. A real girl. Never minding her wide-set eyes, zigzagging legs, and prehensile tail; Clive was starting to see her as human. He had been yearning to welcome someone new into their lives for such a long time, and although Dren was not what he had in mind, he realized that he was glad she was here.

Clive gazed down at her face as she closed her eyes, blissing out as the music built to its climax. In that moment, she was nothing more or less than a lovely young woman. Blushing with pleasure, her ruby lips parted in delight. She was utterly bewitching. His eyes traced the fine line of her jaw and the graceful curve of her neck and found that everything was in its right place. In fact, it all seemed…not only perfect, but perfectly *familiar*. And suddenly, he knew why. A shock shot through him as Dren met his gaze. The thrill he'd felt congealed into a cold lump of dread.

Her eyes glittered at him from between her sooty lashes, sending him an unmistakable message. He recognized it as if from a nightmare. An eerie sense of déjà vu overtook him as he looked down at the creature in his arms. It wasn't just Elsa's dress, Elsa's makeup, and Elsa's jewelry. There was something else, almost like a smell, something intimate and pheromonal that caused his heart to race. He felt as if he had taken a bite of a ripe red apple, only to find a worm twisting in its core. All at once, he achieved a devastating understanding.

"Elsa."

Clive came to a halt and released his partner. His arms dangled limply at his sides and his jaw hung open in horror. A frown crossed her face, but she let out another joyful giggle and tried to throw herself at him. It did her no good.

"That's enough. That's enough dancing, Dren."

She cocked her head this way and that, pouting, making little solicitous coos, but the jig was up. Clive turned on his heels and beat a hasty retreat, leaving Dren in the literal dust, wondering what she could have done wrong.

"Goodnight."

Elsa trudged into the kitchen, rubbing her eyes. In the afternoon light, she blearily perceived Clive's shadow on the other side of the dining room table as she fished a bottle of spring water out of the mess that had collected on the counter. Their semblance of domesticity had quickly dissolved into a kind of collegiate chaos. Dirty dishes, stained coffee mugs, empty fast food cartons, and half-eaten snacks clustered around bags of wilting vegetables and raw grains. Dren was usually the only one to get any fresh food. Elsa filled a glass from the water bottle and turned to Clive.

"Thought I was taking a quick nap," she yawned. "I must have slept like a rock."

There came no reply. Elsa took a cautious step toward her partner and felt the fine hairs on the back of her neck stand up. He was still as a statue, but he hummed with a hostile energy that stopped her in her tracks. She struck a nonchalant pose as she braced for whatever was coming.

"What?"

The whites of Clive's eyes flashed in the dark as he met her gaze. This would be no ordinary lovers' spat. Elsa fought to maintain her air of friendly perplexity, but she could not stop the blood draining from her face as Clive finally said, so low she almost couldn't hear him, the words she had dreaded all this time:

"It's your DNA."

"What?" she replied innocently.

"In Dren. I can tell."

A wave of nausea struck Elsa in the gut. She searched herself for something to say and came up blank. *I knew this was coming eventually,* she thought as she fought to compose herself. *Now it's here. The big talk. I can handle this.* However, the shameful reality was that she had convinced herself that the big talk would never arrive. She had told herself they'd let the fetus grow to term, just for proof of concept. But, of course, she wanted more. She had protected the growing organism all the way through to birth, protected it still after it nearly killed her. She coerced Clive into staying the course in the name of science while she herself went beyond, raising their creation like a child. Then she told herself, and him, that accelerated aging would kill their black market baby before anyone was the wiser. She had convinced Clive that they would never have to explain Dren to the rest of the world, and at the same time, she had convinced herself that she would never have to confess what she had done on her own.

She had become a mother.

Elsa analyzed Clive's posture, his breath, his burning gaze as she tried to prepare a defense. None would come. The love of her life, and the potential father of her purely theoretical children, was now beyond her reach. There was no way out of this.

"You put yourself into the experiment?" He snorted, gestured emptily, almost laughed. "How could you... What were you... I mean, was this ever about science?"

"Of course it was, it still is!" she stammered.

Clive rose abruptly, shaking his head in disbelief. As he began to walk toward the door, he dealt her a devastating blow. "If you really believe that, you're even more fucked up than I think you are."

Elsa's cheeks burned with humiliation, and she began to shake. Where there was once a man who worshiped the ground she walked on, there was now a malevolent stranger charging out of the darkness toward her.

Think of something to say. Quickly!

"What is that supposed to mean?"

Clive stopped in front of Elsa and glowered down at her in open disgust. She felt herself shrinking in his shadow, growing smaller and smaller. She had to put a stop to this, had to turn him around before he left. *Just say something!* She always had something to say, to spin any situation and save herself from defeat. But her agile tongue had turned to wool in her mouth, and her adversary beat her to the punch.

"Maybe you ought to take another look at your family history."

Clive yanked on his coat and threw her one last poisonous look before the front door slammed behind him. Elsa stood there immobilized as the rest of the world seemed to spin around her, faster and faster. She vaguely perceived the sound of the Gremlin turning on and peeling out as she became aware that inside of her, something had broken. Something that wouldn't be fixed.

"Dren?"

Elsa stepped into the barn and padlocked the door behind her with one hand. The other hand supported a large cardboard box with something heavy inside. She looked around for signs of life, and tried to keep her tone light as she called out again.

The fight with Clive left Elsa feeling as if she were bleeding somewhere inside. She had been hollowed out, and dark feelings pooled in the wound: sadness, anger, fear. Vulnerability. At first, Elsa didn't know what to do. Retaliation wasn't an option. What would she even gain by striking back? 'I'm sorry' obviously wasn't going to cut it, either; she wasn't even sure whether it was true. But, sorry or not, she had found herself at the end of everybody's spear. Her scrap with Dren suddenly seemed deadly serious now that she was so entirely friendless. But making up with the hybrid should be easier than getting Clive back, and so Elsa pursued the path of least resistance.

"Dren?" she called out again. She's still in here...right? As she continued her scan for activity, she heard a creaking sound overhead.

High over Elsa's head, Dren stood upright on the worn timber crossbar that had once carried the hay trolley to the loft. Her toes and tail gripped the beam as she stared coldly down at her uninvited guest. Before Elsa could come up with something to say, the creature spread her arms and tipped backward. As if in slow motion, she turned gracefully in the air, and her feet hit the floor with a loud THUD. She advanced with suspicion in her eyes.

Elsa struggled not to show fear. Dren was so powerful now, and apparently free of the desire to please. She would have to tread lightly. She casually sank into an old love seat and set her cargo on the floor before her.

"Hey, Dren! I have something for you," she said blithely. "Come here. I want to give you something."

Dren's tail twitched behind her as she stalked toward Elsa. She towered over the seated human like an enormous mantis.

"Can't you smile for me?" Elsa asked sweetly.

Dren came almost nose to nose with Elsa, studying her face as if it were a counterfeit coin. Elsa imagined Dren taking a bite out of her. Time to get down to business.

"You know I love you, don't you?" Elsa stared into Dren's star-shaped pupils with what she hoped was sincerity.

Dren cocked her head and squinted shrewdly. She knew this word, "love". She also knew there was a difference between the way Clive had said it before, and the way Elsa was saying it now, with such cool deliberation. Elsa forced herself to hold Dren's discerning gaze. *Why was this coming out all wrong?* Elsa searched within herself for the right feeling. She had loved Dren, completely and intensely. She felt it from the moment she'd taken off her gloves and offered her bare palm for the juvenile hybrid to inspect with her delicate feelers. She had loved feeding Dren as she splattered Clive with spit-up and cooed with delight at her first taste of candy. She loved watching Dren grow into a sweet little girl who liked dresses and teddy bears and games that showed off her smarts. Clive was right after all: This wasn't entirely a scientific endeavor for Elsa. It was personal, even spiritual. Maybe in the beginning, Elsa used her own DNA as a point of pride—to brand the project as totally and completely her own. Maybe she was playing God in the grandest sense, creating life in her own image. Or maybe it was all just a matter of loneliness, pure and simple. A strange, irresistible compulsion to bring another Elsa into the world, someone who could understand her. Would make her feel not so different anymore.

"You're a part of me. And I'm a part of you," Elsa insisted. "I'm inside of you."

Maybe it didn't matter why Elsa had done what she did in the beginning. She had fallen in love with Dren. She had experienced the first maternal feelings of her life for the hybrid that was half-herself. This love had changed her, pushed her toward her truest potential. But where was that love now? Why couldn't she make herself feel it? It was as if she'd had to hide it from Clive for such a long time that it had simply vanished.

Dren looked into Elsa's eyes and knew. She knew that what came out of Elsa's mouth didn't match what was in her mind, nor the trembling of her body. Sensing danger, Elsa moved on to her peace offering.

"I have something for you. Look what I got!"

Elsa opened the box, and up popped the head of the docile old barn cat. It meowed gratefully and began to purr as she set it on the floor. It wound itself around its familiar friend's ankles affectionately, but Dren hardly took her eyes off Elsa.

"You can keep her! Why not? It's nice to have a pet."

She forced a smile, but it was too late. Dren glanced disdainfully at Elsa's bribe and, with shocking speed, plunged her stinger into the cat's throat. It howled and twisted like a worm on a hook where she pinned it to the ground. In another breath, it was stone dead. Dren turned her gaze back to Elsa, her lips spread in a malicious grin.

"Oh my god, Dren!"

Elsa lashed out and smacked Dren across the face. It was a full-strength blow that stung her palm and spun the hybrid's head back over her shoulder. A stunned beat passed. Elsa wondered what she had done. *Where had that come from?* Clive's vicious accusation echoed in her mind: *Maybe you ought to take another look at your family history.* But before she could apologize,

Dren knocked the love seat over and crouched over Elsa's chest, her tail waving madly, seeking prey. Its barbed point traced a line from Elsa's chin to her throat before it snapped the chain around her neck. In the blink of an eye, Dren was at the door. She emitted a dreadful cackle as the padlock popped, and the door groaned open.

Sunlight flooded the barn, and Dren was briefly paralyzed with pleasure as its golden warmth poured over her face. But before she tasted freedom again, the rusted head of a shovel landed squarely on the back of her head with all of Elsa's weight behind it. Dren collapsed to the ground, unconscious. And with that, mother and daughter discovered that, despite their biological sameness, they did indeed have irreconcilable differences.

9

A soft, sad twittering alerted Elsa to the fact that her patient was awake. Dren rolled her head this way and that, squinting in the sunbeam that would have to function as a procedure light. She soon discovered that this was the only movement she could make. Elsa stood over her frightened specimen and spoke into her dictaphone.

"Physically, H50 has evolved well. However, recent violent behavior suggests dangerous psychological developments."

Dren lay on her back, lashed to an old wooden worktable by a series of leather straps. Her knees and feet were bound together and drawn to one side, rotating her hips so that her hindquarters were exposed.

"Erratic behavior may be caused by a disproportionate species identification. Cosmetically, human affectation should be eliminated wherever possible."

Elsa set the dictaphone on her instrument cart, freeing her hands to remove the gold locket from around her prisoner's neck. Next, she retrieved a pair of bandage scissors. Dren struggled to hold still as she saw the sharp blades close on the sundress. Elsa sliced each sleeve open before coarsely cutting the dress from collar to hem, and yanking the garment out from under her, leaving her totally exposed. Wadding up the cloth in her fist, Elsa wiped the last traces of makeup from Dren's face. The creature fought to meet Elsa's eyes, pleading for clemency, but to no avail. Elsa remembered how a ferocious barn cat, once cornered and trapped, could suddenly turn sweet and tender as it begged for its freedom.

Clive had hurt Elsa irreparably, but she had taken his advice. Just as he said, she looked back on her family history and saw the truth that she had been ignoring all along. All her life, she had felt so different. A self-sustaining, mold-breaking original whose fate was to be the virgin mother of humanity's future. But despite her glorious destiny, she could not kill the past. For all her disruptive, divergent differences from the rest of the world, way deep down at her very core, Elsa was just like her mother. And at the end of her long battle to break away, she finally came to realize that maybe this wasn't such a bad thing after all. Her mother's austerity, her stoicism, her rejection of feeling; these qualities could have saved Elsa from the predicament in which she now found herself.

In fact, they could save her still. There was still time to prove herself. To prove to Clive that she was still a scientist. To prove to Joan Charot that she would not be held back from the medical breakthrough of the century. To prove to herself that she was still in control. She pushed her cart around to where Dren's twitching tail was tied down by a belt that would double as a tourniquet. Beads of cold sweat stood out on her bare skin, and the musk of her fear mingled with the bracing stench of disinfectant.

"Due to her unstable condition, it has become necessary to remove her zootoxin glands and stinger."

Donning a surgical mask, Elsa loaded a syringe with lidocaine and squeezed off a short spurt into the air. The hybrid seized with agony as Elsa plunged the needle into the tough flesh of her tail. Then Elsa traded her syringe for a scalpel.

The Gremlin pulled up the long dirt road to the barn, its

carapace vibrating with the heavy metal blasting out of its speakers. The drive had done Clive some good, as had his choice of tunes. Among the many things Elsa never understood about his tastes was the fact that harsh noise wasn't just cathartic; it was soothing. When his head swam with frustration and confusion, he turned to the densest, darkest music he could find. The brutal wall of sound flooded his senses, calming his troubled mind.

He was still angry with Elsa—he might be angry for the rest of his life—but now he felt ready to deal with her without immediately sticking his fingers in her deepest wounds. Their relationship may well be over, but the project was not, and they would have to find a way to cooperate to the bitter end. Clive killed the engine. As his soundtrack died, he heard a distinctive howl echo across the barren field. A jolt of panic reawakened his anesthetized nerves. He had been gone too long. Something bad was happening.

He seemed to run toward the barn in slow motion. Time expanded around him as his mind shuffled through a deck of horrific scenarios, each worse than the last. He struggled to stay calm. *Dren is just upset. So is Elsa. So am I. Whatever it is, we can work it out together.* None of these rationalizations penetrated with his reptile brain, which screamed at him with increasing volume to turn away from the barn and never find out what lay within.

Clive pushed open the door and was struck by an unseemly odor. The funk of old sawdust and motor oil now blended with a heady metallic tang that set off deafening alarm bells in his mind. The unforgettable smell of the operating room announced an appalling spectacle: Dren, nude and white as a sheet, was strapped to a table where Elsa stood calmly by in a blood-smeared shop apron.

"What are you doing?"

"What I had to."

Elsa glanced up at him only briefly as she snipped off a strip of medical tape and finished wrapping the red, wet end of Dren's truncated tail. Nearby, in a steel surgical bowl full of ice, lay the last few inches of it, still bleeding out.

"Jesus Christ, Elsa!"

"She's become unstable. She killed the cat. She almost killed me," Elsa explained briskly as she moved the flaccid appendage to a transport cooler.

"So, you cut off her tail?"

Clive could barely raise his voice above a whisper. He felt faint as Elsa snapped off her soiled gloves and dropped them on her instrument cart. Leaving behind a trail of blood-soaked swabs, she picked up the cooler and headed for the exit.

"You any closer to finding the protein?" she asked glibly.

"What does that have to do with anything?"

"You haven't," she said, stopping briefly in front of him, "because you've been working with tissue that's been dead too long."

"You don't know that she has it!"

"Of course she does. She has everything Ginger and Fred have, and more." She threw her coat over her arm and opened the door.

"Where are you going?"

She paused on the threshold for one last, defiant look. "I'm going to solve this thing. I'm going to put things right."

Clive watched helplessly as the door closed behind her. Presently, he heard the Gremlin kick over and pull out. He couldn't be sure how much time passed as he stood there, feeling the walls close in around him. Finally, Dren's miserable moans drew him back to the worktable. He vacillated between pity and revulsion at the sight of her exposed and mutilated body. He covered her with a blanket, as much for his own sake as for hers. He held one of her frigid hands in his before he remembered to undo her bonds.

"I'm sorry. Dren, I —"

His instinct was to try to hold and caress her, but as soon as she was free, she curled into a ball on the table. She could not be reached.

———

Clive filled his whiskey glass for the umpteenth time that night. He had stopped keeping track hours ago and had given up marking time as well. It was clear that Elsa would be gone overnight, which was fine with him. He paced miles around the arctic living room, wishing for a fire to spontaneously ignite in the long-dormant hearth. He could almost hear Elsa's mysterious mother laughing at him from the expressionistic shadows cast by her cockeyed old lamps, and he had begun to feel as cold and dead as she was. The liquor had done little for his mood, but he was grateful for the radiating warmth that spread from his gullet as he greedily gulped it down.

After Elsa left and the sun went down, he was trapped in an endless series of imaginary arguments with her. After years of intellectual sparring—something that used to be a reliable turn-on—Clive had internalized Elsa's powerful voice so deeply that he couldn't win a fight with her even in his fantasies. She was tough to beat on the best of days, but now she was so far gone that no rationale could possibly compel her. Who had she become? He kept seeing her steely gaze again, hearing her inhuman tone ringing out in the barn, and remembering the sickening sight of the amputated tail, once so alive and expressive, bleeding out into the bowl of ice. He fought the urge to vomit.

Poor Dren. He should be doing something for her, but what? His attempts to console her had met with rejection, and eventually he was forced to leave her there, all by herself. Guilt tainted whatever righteous indignation he felt toward Elsa. Something had been profoundly wrong from the very beginning of this nightmare, and Clive had stood by impotently as Elsa steered them unerringly toward catastrophe. Time and time again he could have intervened, could have saved them all, but he had only lapsed deeper into self-pity. He sneered as Elsa disappeared into her bizarre dream of maternity and rolled his eyes smugly when Dren inevitably rejected her overbearing mother. Just like an ordinary teenage girl.

A disarming feeling of tenderness caught him off guard as he pictured Dren all alone in the barn. He slugged back another shot of whiskey, and a strange thought crossed his mind: If he had been more accepting of Elsa's emotional journey—whatever it was—could this disaster have been averted? If he had been less judgmental of her obvious feelings for Dren, no matter how they turned his stomach, would Dren still be in one piece tonight? He had accused Elsa of making their project personal, of being unprofessional, but he knew what his real problem was. He was jealous. She'd shut him out of the parenting process, choosing immaculate conception over his paternal contribution. And then at some point, they had switched places; Dren had turned to him for protection as Elsa became increasingly authoritarian. And Clive had done nothing to stop what was happening. In fact, he had enjoyed it.

He sank into an old wooden chair and woke up his laptop. Logging into his security software, he clicked through the feeds from each of the eight cameras he had rigged up around the barn. He almost asked himself if the stream had frozen as he toggled between the eerily still images of the seemingly empty building when he finally found her. She floated at the bottom of the pasteurization vat, gyrating in the greenish light. A flood of shame chased the visceral pleasure he felt at the sight of her nude body undulating on his monitor. She was as lithe and feminine as her mother, but her uncanniness somehow enhanced her beauty, lending it a special power. A voice from the back of Clive's mind begged him to look away, told him this was wrong, insisted that this was even incestuous somehow. But he simply could not avert his gaze from the body that twisted gracefully in the water.

Then her eyes met his. Or rather, they seemed to. Of course she couldn't really see him studying her from the other end of the video feed; that was absurd. And yet a knowing, deliberate smile played on her lips as she drifted closer. His eyes widened. He must be dreaming it all. And if he were dreaming, well, then there was nothing to feel guilty about. Without thinking, he reached toward the screen, as if he could stroke her cheek.

And her fingers met his.

Clive leapt out of his seat, gasping in horror. Was it a nightmare, after all? She still hovered before his camera with that accusing grin. He shut down his laptop and drained his glass for the final time. Better call it a night.

Elsa emerged triumphantly from the darkened laboratory, shaking out a handful of self-congratulatory candies. After everything she'd done that night, she deserved a little treat. Truth be told, though, work had been rewarding in and of itself. She wasn't even tired. As the sun rose on a new day, she felt more alive than she had in a long time. More herself, in fact. She had been spinning out of control for weeks on end, letting the reins of her life slip through her fingers as she was humiliated and manipulated by the very people who she was supposed to be able to trust. Then, in a single night and by her wits alone, she had turned it all around. She could see the light at the end of the tunnel now, and nothing was going to stop her from reaching the end of this fateful misadventure.

Or at least, that was what she was thinking when she looked up to find Barlow in the vestibule with her, hanging up his overcoat. For a moment, she imagined that he might actually be happy to see her back at the office. Instead, he made a face as if he smelled something foul.

"Bill, you're early!" she chirped.

He didn't miss a beat. "Let me get this straight. You stay

home because you're sick, and now I find you sneaking around while no one's here."

"Making up for lost time," she said around a mouthful of candy.

"It's too late for that," Barlow declared furiously. "They won't extend the deadline. It's over. You…you screwed us all!"

He stared her down, waiting for her sense of culpability to sink in. He would have to wait a long time. Elsa was suppressing laughter as she watched Barlow's cheeks redden. He forged ahead anyway.

"In fact, while you're here, why don't you clear out Clive's desk?"

"I don't think so," she replied casually, still crunching on clusters of sugar.

"Well, no one cares what you think anymore," Barlow parried. Elsa could hardly contain herself as he straightened his back, puffing himself up like a cornered animal. "You're an embarrassment to this company. It's going to take us years—"

"The protein has been synthesized," said Elsa serenely.

She swept past him to the exit, stopping on the threshold for one last stab at him. Somehow, this had turned into one of the best days of Elsa's life.

"It's in the fridge! When some real scientists get here, have them take a look."

"Ouch."

Clive opened his eyes just long enough to learn that he didn't want to do that. His head throbbed, bitterly resisting consciousness, and it felt like his joints had fused together overnight. He would have remained folded up under his winter coat on the old couch if the events of the previous day hadn't come creeping back to mind. He lay still for another moment, listening for evidence of life. The farmhouse was silent, though he couldn't guess whether Elsa had snuck up to bed yet. *At least I don't hear any screaming,* he told himself, but the thought woke him up properly. He had to check on Dren.

The barn door groaned its familiar greeting as Clive opened the padlock and stepped inside. He had come directly from the couch, forgetting his coat in his haste. He didn't have a plan for what to do if Dren had found another escape route, but he had to find out if she had. He rubbed his hands together briskly and stuffed them into his armpits as he surveyed his troublingly silent surroundings.

"Elsa?" It wasn't who he most hoped to see, but he'd rather not be surprised.

There came not a sound. He was wondering whether or not he should feel relieved, when something near him stirred. A primitive, indefinable sense of presence climbed his spine like a ladder to where the hairs on the back of his neck stood on end. Perhaps he felt the air move, just on the edges of his perception. Maybe he heard a sound that was barely a sound, like something fluttering or slithering behind him. There might have been a smell that was not quite a smell, just the animal sense that something near you is alive. Though his harried survival instincts cried out against it, he forced himself to turn around.

There stood Dren, naked, with her arms outstretched. She was radiantly beautiful. Her diaphanous wings shimmered in the sun, and the fishlike fins stood up proudly between her shoulder blades. Clive was paralyzed by the sight of her. Which, perhaps, was exactly the point. Just as his eyes came to rest on hers, she flung herself at him. The wings vanished into her body with a slippery sound as she wrapped her arms around his neck and pressed her lips to his. He felt himself kissing her back before he had time to think.

"No, no!" he cried, pressing her firmly backward. "You can't do that!"

She was instantly mortified. The creature who had just mesmerized him with her mating display now covered herself modestly and whimpered tragically. As if in a trance, Clive saw himself reaching out to comfort her.

"You shouldn't do that," he said in a passable impression of paternal concern.

He stroked the back of her head as she sulked, to soothe her, he told himself, but it wasn't the truth. As his skin touched hers, she looked up into his eyes. He cupped her warm cheek in his palm and found himself frozen like a deer in headlights. He was still shaking his head "no" as the distance closed between them.

"You shouldn't do that," he repeated softly as her lips met his.

It happened so naturally. Clive, his mind, his morals, were not a part of the process. Dren pressed herself to him tightly, as if she could penetrate him, become him. Now she led the dance, kissing him passionately as she walked him backward until he hit the wooden stairs to the pasteurization vat. She threw one leg over his hip and the remaining length of her mangled tail whipped itself around a stair, trapping him against the vat. He had nowhere to go as he heard that hair-raising rattle rise from within her, along with a feral growl. He had absolutely no idea how much trouble he was in.

Dren regarded her prey with obvious pleasure, enjoying his paralysis, but wanting more. She fell to the floor beneath him, giving him back his power. Her feigned submission activated him. He was barely conscious of freeing his erection from his jeans before he had plunged himself into her to the hilt. Her prehensile toes dug into his sweater and slid it over his head as he began to fuck her in earnest. He pushed into her with his full weight, enjoying his temporary dominance of the powerful creature before she deftly flipped her slave onto his back and sat astride him with her wings, forming a canopy over his head. An otherworldly, almost musical purr cascaded from her mouth as she took what she wanted from him.

Clive's precious intellect had abandoned him completely. There, on the dusty floor of the barn, he had become more animal than Dren. His hands mapped her body, pawing her perfect breasts, grasping at her slender hips. He closed his eyes, and, through his fingertips, he saw the magnified surface of her hairless skin. Something like ego death overcame him, and he lost all awareness of the difference between her body and his. She allowed him to turn her on her back again and, as he labored over her mindlessly, he heard a strange, visceral sound. He would not have to find out that Dren's tail had regenerated, along with its baneful spine. Before he could look over his shoulder to find it hovering behind his head, his eyes settled on something far worse.

In their cluttered little ersatz house, where antiques mingled with industrial scrap, there stood a pane of glass, leaned against a wooden beam. In that piece of glass, Clive could see an unexpected shaft of sunlight enter the barn, and in that shaft of sunlight stood a familiar silhouette.

Before Clive was even off his knees, Elsa was flying across the field to the Gremlin. He gave chase with his pants hanging around his hips, reaching her just as she turned the key in the ignition. The tires spun, spraying his bare chest with snow, before the car took off like a shot and vanished from sight.

Clive pulled the van cautiously through the driving snow toward their apartment building. As he turned toward the underground garage, he spotted the toxic orange Gremlin parked out front. At least he knew where she was. It had been the longest drive of his life. The distance between the farmhouse and their long-empty home had seemed to telescope infinitely before him, giving him time to think—something that, for once in his life, he did not want. He would not be forgiven for the unforgivable, but still, he owed Elsa a statement. But what could he say? He couldn't tell her what he was thinking because he simply wasn't thinking. He was barely aware of his surroundings when she had walked in on them. He could almost have blamed Dren, for all they knew about her.

Maybe she had exerted some pheromonal control over him. Maybe there was something in her saliva, transferred to him with a kiss, that lowered his defenses, severing his connection to reality. Maybe she contained, among other medical miracles, an aphrodisiac compound of the mythical kind that so many rhinoceri had died for. In West India, an alkaloid from the Bufo toad was used in a dangerous but sought-after preparation called "love stone"; why couldn't Dren produce some similar secretion? That could account for a sensible man like Clive flinging himself into the arms of something not altogether human. Something that he knew, by then, was his lover's daughter.

The thought soured his stomach. He knew he was deflecting blame, but it was hard to avoid. Dren was just as angry with Elsa as he was. She had every reason to want revenge. She had been imprisoned, tortured, and disfigured by her heartless mother. She had seen how Elsa tortured Clive, too, in a subtler sense; how he too was confined and deprived of what he needed. Dren had known just how to seduce Clive. Part of her was still a woman, after all. Maybe Clive wasn't a co-conspirator for Dren, but rather a trophy, something she could take from Elsa to hurt her in a much deeper way than mere flesh would allow.

Clive killed the engine and gave himself a shake, as if he could dislodge the thought. He was still scapegoating Dren, projecting onto the creature complex, adult, human notions that were in no way provable parts of her psyche. It seemed like he couldn't stop blaming her for his own behavior. He reminded himself that she was just an animal. An animal who had pushed her slender, pointed tongue into his mouth, who spread her wings over his head as she slid herself down onto his neglected cock. He fought the impulse to start the van back up and leave. Go find a bridge somewhere and jump off. Any fate seemed preferable to the one he now faced. At length, he forced himself to leave the vehicle and head for their floor.

At the door, key in hand, he hesitated. One last chance to get my story straight, he thought, before remembering that there was no story. He had no excuse. Elsa would say whatever she needed to say to him before they would decide together how to bring this surreal drama to some sort of logical conclusion. That was the most important thing. And there was no sense putting it off any longer. He entered the apartment.

When he found the courage to lift his eyes, he saw Elsa sitting at their dining room table, facing the door as if she had been waiting for him to arrive for his appointment. Cognitive dissonance set in. His beautiful friend, their warm, familiar home, their beloved possessions, their collective smell, all made his head swim with the desire to collapse. He could have swept her up in his arms and taken her directly to bed, to sleep side by side until the whole situation somehow resolved itself without them. But the look on Elsa's face brought him back to reality.

"El—"

"Don't." Her eyes burned through him. She repelled him with a raised palm. "Don't."

He removed his coat, as if to prevent her from ejecting him. "I don't even quite know how it happened. I was barely—"

"I don't even know who you are anymore," she said. She looked pale and weak. Her eyes were red and damp and her voice shook, yet she was implacable. "You've become something sick. Forget about what it means to me. There are some things you do not do!"

He forced himself to hold her gaze, though he felt it might turn him to salt. Finally, he said the one true thing he could think of.

"We changed the rules."

She practically burst into flame. "You're not talking your way out of this!"

Clive began to pace. The corners of his mouth twitched, and

he rubbed his temples compulsively as he searched for a summary of what had happened. "We crossed a line. Things got confused."

"Confused about what?"

Elsa's willful ignorance revived the indignation that had fueled Clive for so long before he had foolishly forfeited the high ground. He stopped in his tracks and looked her in the eye. The answer should have been obvious.

"Right and wrong."

He picked up his coat. This was going nowhere. He shouldn't have come.

"Right and wrong. Do you have any idea how naïve that sounds?" Fresh tears streamed down her cheeks. "You're in no position to talk to me about right and wrong!"

Clive slammed the coat onto the floor, startling Elsa out of her tirade. He shouldn't have to apologize to her. And he wasn't going to. Not anymore.

"And you are? Really?" he shouted hoarsely. He stormed up to her and glared down into her face. "Why the fuck did you want to make her in the first place? Huh? For the betterment of mankind?"

Elsa was stunned into silence. She shuddered, her eyes welled, but she said nothing. Clive had her where he wanted her, and he struck.

"You never wanted a normal child. Because you were afraid of losing control. But an experiment…that's something else!"

As he turned his back on her, he heard a very small voice.

"I love her."

Heartbreak nearly swallowed him up. He couldn't hate Elsa. He hurt for her, and for himself. But he couldn't relent.

"Yeah, I know. But we fucked up, El! We fucked up. Jesus Christ." He chose not to privilege her with the sight of his tears. "We've chained her up. We locked her away from the world. We maimed her!"

"I maimed her."

Elsa's voice shattered like glass. She had stuffed her humanity way down deep inside herself to prove to Clive that she was still a scientist, that she was capable of any indecency to further their agenda, and now it was bursting back through the surface. Clive spared himself the spectacle of her agony, lest it push him over the edge.

"I just wish things could go back to the way they were," he sighed to the ceiling.

The silence was stifling. Only Elsa's delicate sniffles moved the air. She was the first to speak.

"I synthesized the protein."

"What?"

She cleared her throat, trying to shift back to neutral. "She has a derivative. It's more stable than CD356. It's ten times higher than the level that Ginger and Fred ever had."

Something in Clive returned to life. He seated himself across from Elsa, scratching his chin. They eyed each other hopefully.

"We could maybe save things," he whispered. "I don't mean us. I mean…"

Darkness descended upon the room. A chill shook them both. Clive watched as the grim realization settled over Elsa's features. He prayed she wouldn't argue. He couldn't let her.

"Oh, God. We can't do that," she gasped. "We can't. We have a responsibility."

But the fight had gone out of her. Clive knew it. He shook his head.

"The experiment is over. Our responsibility is to end it."

10

The sun was setting on the farm as the Gremlin crawled down the dirt road to the barn. The cawing of crows greeted them as they stepped out of the car into the balmy air. The snow had stopped falling, and the weather warmed just enough to create an oppressive humidity that seemed to expand in Elsa's lungs, suffocating her. However long Clive's trip from the farm to their apartment had been, Elsa's journey home had been much, much longer.

Grief was not something at which Elsa was practiced. For a child born into lack, everything was a gain. She had never mourned a loved one. She had skillfully avoided anything that threatened a negative return on investment, including demanding relationships and dalliances that might drain her precious energy. Everything was in the service of her brilliant career, including Clive, to some degree. He had added his impressive processing power to hers, and provided her with the creature comforts that, she had to admit, increased her productivity when properly balanced against work. *Who will make sure I don't eat candy for dinner?* she wondered morosely before brushing the thought away. The loss of his love hadn't fully crystallized in her mind yet, but she couldn't deal with it now.

She hadn't much of a choice anyway. A much more immediate loss was rushing toward her.

They entered the barn into a disquieting stillness. Even when Dren was hiding, Elsa always sensed her presence. Call it a maternal instinct. It may not have been very scientific of her, but Elsa had learned to trust this surprising awareness of where her child was, how she felt, what she needed. Now Dren's absence was stunning. The non-vibration of the void jarred Elsa. She didn't want to do what had to be done, but Dren's escape would make their burden infinitely worse.

"Dren!"

"Dren? Come out, Dren."

They kept their voices calm and casual, even though Dren was capable of perceiving deception with an acuity that was almost psychic. Clive crept among Dren's toys, peeking under a sheet to find only piles of plush animals. The loft was clear. The stalls were empty. Not a creature was stirring. If Dren were there, she could surely hear Elsa's heart beating to break her ribs. They continued to call out as Elsa climbed the stairs to the edge of the pasteurization vat.

"Dren?"

Elsa's blood froze in her veins. The water was still and opaque, suggestive of stagnation, but something much less natural had taken place. A thick, greenish film had spread over the basin, and it emitted a weird smell whose character was simply not in Elsa's vocabulary. Panic crawled up her spine as she leaned over the lip of the vat and reached out to touch the unctuous fluid. And then, she beheld a horror she would not forget the rest of her life.

"Clive!"

"What?"

He arrived at Elsa's side to find out what she saw in the brackish pool. Viscous strands of bacterial bubbles crisscrossed the submerged face of their grand experiment. Dren's unblinking eyes stared up at them damningly. Her high, round cheeks were slack and waxen, and white as marble. She moved not an inch. It appeared that her executioners had arrived too late.

Clive and Elsa lay Dren's dead weight carefully down on her bed, covering her to the chin with an afghan. She had not yet expired, but her time seemed imminent. Her chest still rose and fell, though almost imperceptibly, and a soft wheezing escaped her bluish lips. The pair sat on either side of Dren's funeral bier, dabbing her face with a cloth, and stroking her pale forehead.

"What's happening?"

"I don't know," Clive whispered. "But she's dying."

Hours passed that may as well have been days. A shaft of sun from the skylight passed slowly across Dren's weakening body. Clive slumbered in his chair across from Elsa who knelt, painfully penitent, and wept into the afghan.

Dren never awoke to absolve her.

Clive was roused by the sharpening sound of Elsa's cries. His eyes opened on a body whose mortality was unmistakable. He came to stand over his kneeling partner. Her golden hair hid her face as her delicate fingers spread across the soft knit shroud. Her grief was fathomless.

By some unknown hour of the night, Dren's body lay at the bottom of a hole, as deep as they could dig it in the winter earth. The unseasonable warmth had been a stroke of luck, the only one they'd had for quite a while; much of the snow remained, and the cold still slowed their muscles, but they had been able to break ground. Their breath swirled in the moonlight as they looked down at the bundle of blankets below their feet. Elsa gingerly placed her Barbie Doll in the grave alongside the departed. This death, which they had planned and failed to enact themselves, was too great a thing, their guilt too outrageous to comprehend. With the slow murder of their unnatural child, they had crossed out of the world they once knew, into an exile from which they would never return.

"Do you, uh…want to say anything?" Clive offered weakly.

Elsa shook her head.

Clive hauled another wheelbarrow full of evidence out to the pyre before the barn. It was like a small house fire: The broken down remains of Dren's bed, the vanity, the stroller full of toys—everything she had touched was slowly turning to ash. Clive held her favorite teddy bear in his hands as if it were some arcane relic, trying to name the feeling it gave him. He remembered how it looked when it was new, when its arrival had filled him with frustration. Now it was matted and worn from Dren's faithful love. It had provided him and Elsa with a curious meter for their creation's development. The teddy seemed big in the arms of little Dren, almost her size, the perfect friend; an anthropomorphized animal like herself. In the bed of big Dren, it was a reminder of her growing maturity, and conversely, of her unchanging innocence. The toy horse of Kaspar Hauser. He cast it into the flames.

The last thing to go was Elsa's old makeup kit, which had become Dren's. It felt radioactive in Clive's hands. Its existence gave him a feeling of alienation that he could not have described, even if anyone were listening. There was something about the particular privacy of girls. Boys thrived on prideful exhibitionism, but girls' natural secrecy, their lives lived through coded documents and symbologies, seemed to be the key to their survival. With a strange feeling of disgust, Clive threw it into the fire. He had considered opening the box after Elsa gave it to him for disposal. He had the passing thought that somewhere inside it was an explanation, an exhibit A that would decode her unspoken thoughts and feelings, her unknowable past, and the selfish sins that had led them both to this moment. But he left it intact before burning it with the rest. There was nothing there, nothing anywhere, that would explain anything at all.

Elsa continued to move all the evidence of their presence into a centralized pile in the barn where it could be easily loaded into the wheelbarrow. Though they had lived there only a short while, the task felt like a Sisyphean nightmare. Her stiffening joints creaked as she clutched yet another hunk of antique carpentry to her chest, arching her back to keep it airborne until she reached her destination. Her back had just about had it though, and she stumbled, dropping the chest of drawers on its face. Exhaustion rose up and consumed her; despair beckoned seductively. Giving up was immensely appealing, but she gritted her teeth and righted the chest. As she did, one of its drawers slid out, and produced a small stack of loose papers.

Elsa turned them over in her hands. Dren's drawings. Not the ones of Clive, which she later saw as a portent of the awful things to come. These were drawings Elsa didn't get to see, that she might have seen if she hadn't intruded on Dren's privacy. *Are there any of me?* she had asked, a question that seemed to send the hybrid into a rage. Here they were: Elsa as a little blonde stick person. Elsa with eyes, lips, and a nose. Elsa with clothes. Elsa's distinctive heart-shaped face, her makeup, jewelry she really owned. Each image grew in detail, a sense of intimacy, and an undeniable affection.

Tears poured helplessly down Elsa's cheeks as she set the drawings aside without looking where they lay. She saw nothing before her. Felt nothing but an all-eclipsing blackness. She might never have come back from it if Clive hadn't returned at that moment to collect a fresh haul.

"Almost done?"

She straightened her back and brushed away her tears hastily. "Yeah, almost."

Clive wrapped his arms around a large box of toys and made for the door, when the sound of a motor and gravel under rubber froze them where they stood.

"You hear that?"

"Yeah."

Barlow's sedan came to a stop in front of their bonfire. The passenger door opened, and the beam of Clive's flashlight illuminated Gavin's face. His cheeks were hollow, eyes sunken but full of urgency.

"Wha— Gavin, what are you doing here?"

Clive's little brother walked into the light of the fire, projecting an uncharacteristic gravity.

"I'm sorry. I had to," he declared. "It was the only way."

He looked back over his shoulder at Barlow, who emerged from the vehicle full of wrathful pomposity. He stormed up to the edge of the fire.

"All right!" he shouted. "Let's see it."

Elsa ignored him, fixated on Gavin. "What did you tell him?"

"I didn't have to tell him much."

Barlow wouldn't be dismissed. "You think I'm stupid? The samples you gave me had human DNA content. They didn't come from Ginger and Fred. They came from something else, something that's still alive."

Elsa could have been brought to ground by her own hubris, humiliated by her blind assumption that no one would notice something so stark and simple that even Barlow could see it. Clive's rage could have reached its peak, and he could have thrown his treacherous partner to the wolves. But by this time, they had been through something that their petty, pathetic project manager couldn't possibly imagine. Now, when he finally had them pinned to the wall, he seemed smaller to them than he ever had before.

Still, Barlow blustered on, gaining steam. "And to think you did this on my watch! Now, let's see this thing. It doesn't belong to you."

"'It' doesn't belong to anyone," Clive replied calmly.

"Where is it?" Barlow nearly screamed. He waited. He would have to wait forever. "Fine. I'm calling a forensic team."

He reached for his phone just as Elsa came to life, casually brushing past him to the other side of the fire.

"She's already dead. It's over."

Barlow looked from Elsa to Clive and back, destabilized by this information.

"I don't believe you!" he proclaimed haughtily.

"No?" Elsa replied as she turned back to him with a shovel in her hands. "Well, see for yourself. She's buried behind the barn."

Elsa tossed Barlow the shovel as he gazed at her in confusion. His mouth twitched as he tried to think of a retort—one that would never come. A violent gust of wind shot up from the earth itself, blasting over Elsa's head from the shadows behind her. She covered her face as detritus from the forest floor scoured her parka, and when she opened her eyes again, Barlow had disappeared. He had left behind only a primal scream, creating an anti-harmony with an eldritch screech that echoed down from the tops of the trees. He and his captor had vanished before the dust hit the ground.

The three remaining scientists stared helplessly into the night sky. The ensuing silence was broken by the sounds of branches rending and snapping somewhere in the darkness. Courageously, and very foolishly, Gavin ran headlong toward the sound. Elsa and Clive gave chase. They didn't have far to go.

Clive pointed his flashlight up at the top of an ancient oak where, some twenty feet in the air, William Barlow's lifeless body hung from the naked branches. They could just make out his face in the beam, white streaked with glistening red, frozen in a final moment of unknown horror.

"Oh, shit…" Clive whispered.

The reply was a low, guttural roar that rattled the very ground under their feet. Clive spun around, turning his beam in the direction of the sound. Their eyes followed it up to the barn's peaked roof, where they were met with a shocking sight.

"What the fuck is going on?"

Clive shook from head to toe, gasping for air. Compulsively, he looked to Elsa for guidance, but none would come. Dren had returned, but not the Dren they knew. The creature that stood over them with its wings spread imperiously was still Elsa's only child—but it was no longer the daughter she had known and loved. This was now Elsa's son. Pale, piercing eyes smoldered under a dramatically ridged brow. High cheekbones pitched out over a heavy, square jaw. Bands of muscle ran along his neck to its powerful shoulders, from which spread dragon-like wings stretched across cartilaginous spines terminating in deadly points. He was the vision of William Blake come to terrifying life.

"Dren?" Elsa whispered. Dren heard.

With another devastating bellow, the creature vanished over the peak of the roof. But it didn't go far.

They couldn't see it, but they could sense it. The thing swirled over their heads in ever-narrowing circles. The three humans tried to move as one, turning this way and that to spot the oncoming threat. The hulking mass swooped before them with a malevolent shriek, then behind them, its wake throwing clouds of dirt and dead leaves into their faces. They twisted in the wind, struggling to stay together. And then suddenly, three became two.

Gavin's last words were simply his brother's name. The ragged syllable echoed through the pines, away from Clive, who would never hear his sibling's voice again.

Clive took off at a sprint. He ran blindly through the dark woods, the world becoming a black and white blur in the beam of his flashlight. He screamed and cried. He begged for Gavin to return. He heard nothing but his own voice. Elsa chased after him hopelessly, imploring him to stop. She knew he never would.

Clive and Elsa had lived a lifetime in the blink of an eye. Parenthood, divorce, the loss of a child. It was impossible to imagine that they could suffer still more. Yet, they would find ways.

"Clive, stop!"

"*Gavin!*"

"We have to go back!"

Bare branches tore at Clive's face, slowing him just enough for Elsa to catch up. She closed in on him as he spun in circles, his flashlight finding nothing in the trees. The light glinted off a stagnant pond, all around which were unbreachable brambles. Elsa put her hands on Clive, trying to steady him as he sputtered deliriously, still searching for signs of life.

"Clive, we have to go back!"

"I can't, I have to—I can't!" Clive's tongue could barely form words, but his body would not relent.

"Look, he's gone," Elsa panted. She gripped his arms with all her might, struggling to stay in his line of sight. "We can't stay here, okay? *It's* out there!"

With no way forward, Clive finally began to slow down. His eyes focused on Elsa.

"What happened?"

"Ginger," she explained hastily. "It's the same thing that happened with Fred and Ginger. Okay, now let's go!"

She pulled him in the direction of the farm, but he shook her off.

"I'm not leaving my brother!"

"He's dead, okay?" she cried. "He's already dead!"

"I'm not leaving my brother!" he howled with renewed mania.

"Let's go!"

Elsa yanked on his arm to spin him around, and his flashlight flew into the murky pond. Its light shrank rapidly to a dim glow somewhere at the bottom.

"No!"

Clive plunged a fallen branch into the water, desperately feeling for the flashlight's handle. Elsa hung from his shoulders, dragging him back from the edge with all her strength, but it was simply not enough.

"Just let it go!"

"I need it!" Clive gasped senselessly. "We need it!"

He bellied down on the rotten deadfall ringing the pond, reaching deeper into its depths with his branch. Elsa withdrew; her added weight could sink them both. She watched in horror as the love of her life slid further toward the black water.

"Almost...almost have it...," he grunted.

And then, at the moment of his victorious cry—*I got it!*—Clive was sucked into the shallows where he swiftly sank out of sight. The foul water rushed in to fill the void he left behind, gobbling him up. The thing had been waiting down there to receive him.

Elsa crouched on all fours at the edge of the deadfall, making sounds. Most of were simply his name. Some were cries.Others were deranged giggles. A gasping, rasping hiccup stretched her voice in ways she herself had never heard. She barked and screamed at the water, ordering it to surrender him. For a long time, no answer came. The water was almost still.

And then, Clive returned. He breached the surface, coughing up swamp water, steam pouring from his skin.

"Clive! Grab my hand!"

Elsa lunged toward him, gripping the ground with one hand and his waterlogged parka with the other. She pried him from the embrace of his watery grave and, once he was on land, turned him on his back.

"Okay, now get up, because we need to go. We need to go, now!" Clive's strength was failing him. There was mud in his lungs and ice in his veins. She shook him and shook him, to no avail. He coughed weakly and a stream of silty water ran from the corners of his mouth, but his eyes did not open. Elsa stammered mindlessly. "I know. It's OK, it's OK, it's OK..."

The water stirred again.

Elsa looked up from her dying lover to see something emerge from the roiling pond that could have been a Greek statue. His ivory flesh shone in the moonlight as he broke the surface and unfurled like a fern, his broad chest gleaming as his wings slithered out of the rents in his body. There he paused, displaying himself as if for her pleasure.

She was not seduced. As Elsa flung herself into the treeline, she heard Dren explode out of the water with a harrowing war cry. She careened through the dead branches that scored her face, doing her best to run in a straight line toward what she hoped was the farm. It couldn't last long. She looked over one shoulder and then the other to see if the thing was still behind her, and before she knew it, she had no idea where she was. In desperation, she squeezed herself into the snarled undergrowth and waited.

There was little she could do to steady her breathing. Her blood sang in her ears. She thought she must be making an enormous amount of noise, but she could not stop. She gripped the brambles around her, lest he try to tear her out of them. She waited longer still.

After an eternity, Elsa felt the air move around her. Nimble footsteps circled her hiding place. Unthinking, she broke out of the thicket and sprinted into the shadows. Over her head, a hideous dinosauric yowl bounced off the trees, seeming to come from everywhere at once. Something deep in her bones told her she was done for, but she could not stop running. Like all animals, she would die striving to live.

The flapping of leathery wings met her ears, rapidly growing louder. Her feet moved faster than ever before—and carried her face-first into a fallen tree.

When Elsa opened her eyes, the first thing she saw was Dren's face. He straddled her hips and held her wrists out to her sides. Up close, it struck her that he was just as beautiful as her daughter had been, could be even more beautiful to her now, were death not so primally repulsive. He sniffed at her, sticking his muzzle into the hollow of her neck. She felt his hot, damp breath on her cold flesh. Blood dripped from her forehead into her eyes, but she could not close them, could not let him out of her sight, even if he was the last thing she ever saw.

A brute growl came from the core of Dren, shaking Elsa's bones as he sat astride her. Then, faster than she could see, he slashed open her clothing down to her bare skin. Down feathers fluttered in the moonlight between her and the creature as he cackled, a bi-tonal bleating sound that was somehow as familiar to her as it was cold and alien. She screamed without knowing it. A single, senseless question escaped her lips:

"WHAT DO YOU WANT?"

She snatched back a shred of sanity with her words—the desire to know; her deepest impulse as a person, as a scientist. She sobbed and squirmed and she might not be able to save her life, but still, she could speak. Still, she was human. She tried again.

"What do you want?"

Dren leaned into her face, studying her features with pleasure. A rattling, buzzing croak boiled up from his depths. It was a sound Elsa had never heard before. He curled his lips around it, manipulating it into weird, new aural shapes. She feared that his mouth would produce some horrible new poison, or weapon, and braced herself for death.

And then, at long last, came Dren's first words.

"INSIDE...YOU."

Clive opened his eyes to nothing. A last-gasp flush of adrenaline coursed through his system, jolting him awake. At first, he was unable to differentiate the dark branches from the darker sky. Then he felt the earth beneath him and remembered.

Elsa!

He shot to his feet. He knew neither his injuries, the sediment in his lungs, nor the deadly cold as he plunged into the tree line. He had to find her, even if it was too late. He followed a strange, muffled commotion to a clearing illuminated by the moon.

What he saw there could have killed him all by itself.

Elsa lay on the ground beneath Dren. They were ringed by a halo of her shredded clothing. He emitted deep, gurgling grunts as he pumped his muscular hips between her splayed thighs. Elsa's eyes pointed blindly up at the sky, cold as marbles. She made involuntary, unconscious sounds. Her body moved only as the creature jostled her with each thrust. She was, mercifully, not there.

A sickening squawk joined Dren's rhythmic grunting, and he threw back his head, eyes closing in the oblivion of climax.

Now was the time.

Clive picked up a fallen branch and, lifting it high above his head, drove it into the center of Dren's back. He threw all of his weight behind it and felt the makeshift stake pass through the creature's entrails and out of its solar plexus.

Elsa was brought back to herself by a hellish wail that tore through the night air. A vague semblance of consciousness returned, refocusing itself on the creature arching above her. Some sort of grotesque new appendage, stiff, ragged, and slick with gore, protruded from the center of his body. Her first thought was that it must be something reproductive. Something erotic. And then he stopped howling and collapsed onto his side with an exhausted rattle. As this happened, she felt something slither out from between her legs. From within her.

The sensation was so shocking that it ripped her out of her protective fugue and spilled her back into brutal reality. She scrambled to her feet only to find that her jeans were torn nearly in half. Something wet and thick clung to her thighs; she could hear it spattering the forest floor beneath her. She had a feeling as if she'd been beaten very badly, somewhere deep inside.

She began to remember why when she saw Clive standing over the impaled Dren, who whined and twitched like a dying insect. *Clive!* He wasn't dead. He had come back for her. He still loved her. He had saved her, and everything was going to go back to the way it was! Just like he said. They were going to be free.

But Dren had not stopped moving. They watched in horror as he reached behind himself and slid the heavy branch out of the hole in his thorax. It fell to the earth with a wet thud. He raised himself up on all fours and glared defiantly up at his assailant. As he hauled himself to his feet, his fearsome wings slithered out with a nauseating noise—or maybe they heard his guts knitting themselves back together, courtesy of the Ambystoma gene his parents had generously gifted him. Dren towered over Clive, huffing like an enraged bull. Suddenly, Clive was on his back again. Dren circled him, wings in full flare, preparing for the death blow. The last of Clive's will was spent. He would not get up again.

And then, just before Dren pounced, he was brought asunder. Elsa stood over her son with a large, heavy rock in her hands. The creature lay at her feet, nearly lifeless. He suddenly seemed so pitiable, lying there naked, blood pouring from a mortal wound on his bare skull. With what little strength he had left, he turned his face toward his mother, to look at her one last time. Elsa looked back. It felt like a thing she had to give him, the last look. The final acknowledgment. He met her gaze frankly, with something almost like acceptance. She had given him life. She would take it away. It was the most natural thing in the world.

And then he struck.

As Dren held Elsa's attention, his tail lashed out and sank its stinger into Clive's heart. It was the last thing he knew. Clive couldn't even react before his body fell limp, his last breath rushing out of him. Elsa could actually see it hanging in the winter air. It floated before her for a fleeting moment, something she could almost have held in her hands: her lover's last breath.

Elsa brought the rock down again. It was all over in seconds. Quietly, matter-of-factly, over. When Dren's body came to rest, Elsa lay on the ground between her child and her best friend. She curled up and waited for death.

"Your *'Dren'* turned out to be...a cauldron of unimaginable mysteries."

Elsa sat in the guest seat in Joan Charot's penthouse office overlooking the city and listened to the Chief Operating Officer describe the past year of her life. The older woman's patented pauses for effect didn't have quite the same weight when you knew how her sentence would end. But Elsa was patient. Joan continued.

"Aside from the intense concentration of CD356 in her system, she was filled with a variety of completely unique compounds. We'll be filing patents for years."

Joan circled Elsa with her hands tucked into the pockets of her elegant smoke-grey blazer, letting her seductive voice trail behind her. There was a time when this performance frightened and excited Elsa, just as it was engineered to do. Now it just seemed perfunctory. The COO came around in front of Elsa and looked her meaningfully in the eye as she sank into her own chair, literally coming down to Elsa's level. Just as Joan once used the enveloping darkness of her boardroom to intimidate Elsa, here she let the sun play over her ageless features to convey comradery.

"Of course, we are extremely excited that you are willing to take us with you to the next stage. Especially in light of the... personal risk."

Elsa could have lip synced along with this line, dramatic pause and all. Still, the wording destabilized her. She didn't remember very much about the incident that brought her here, which she considered a blessing. But whenever she was reminded of it, she felt something squirm inside of her. Something that seemed to know what was happening.

"We think the figure we've come up with is very generous."

Joan pushed a document across the table for Elsa's inspection. What was printed under the Newstead Pharmaceuticals letterhead would have made an ordinary person jump for joy, but she was completely unsurprisable. As she breezed through the fine print, Joan leaned in and attempted to reinforce the gravity of this transaction. Insisting on eye contact, she dropped the corporate mask and projected the full, fatal force of her executive powers.

"You can never speak of this. To anyone. Ever."

Elsa scrawled her name casually, as if she were signing a standard issue HIPAA agreement. She passed the document back to Joan and rose to her feet. With some difficulty. She stood before the COO for just a moment, letting her body speak for her.

Elsa's belly had swelled tremendously. There was simply no predicting how long, or short, the gestation period might be. Each time the baby, if that's what one chose to call it, turned over or kicked, it might signal the start of some strange new process. Her condition required relentless monitoring, considering the speed and violence with which Dren had come out of BETI, destroying the machine in the process. This would frighten Elsa if she had any investment in her future. At least, in the kind of future most people wanted. She crossed to the window and looked out at the metropolis far below, which seemed quite inconsequential from here.

Joan came to stand behind her. Elsa felt the woman's nervous eyes on her back, a sensation she would have enjoyed in another life. Joan seemed to be probing for a reaction to what anyone else would consider an extreme situation. Elsa gave her no such satisfaction.

"Nobody would blame you if you didn't do this. You could just put an end to it and walk away."

Elsa smiled bitterly to herself. She almost laughed. She wondered if she should, if that would do something interesting to Joan Charot. She thought of the many moments spanning all of the time she spent with Dren, when she could have just put an end to it and walked away. How many times she had been begged to do exactly that? And by whom?

"What's the worst that could happen?"

A little private joke, just for Clive. She tried to imagine what he would say if he could see her now. She honestly wasn't sure. Joan placed her hands on Elsa's shoulders patronizingly. She was still searching for something: some emotion or insecurity, a weakness she could exploit to bring them together. She would not find one. Elsa was different from Joan. Joan was a shallow creature, full of the optimistic fantasies of privilege. The dark consequences of her actions were a pure abstraction, a hazy shadow that accentuated the brightness of her success. Whatever sacrifices she made to achieve her position held no enduring meaning for her. As far as she was concerned, the blood on her hands was purely theoretical. She couldn't imagine what darkness lived inside of Elsa, neither metaphorically nor literally.

Joan knew no difference. She appeared exceptional, with her unstoppable accumulation of power, but at her core, she was just like anybody else. She wanted the same things as everybody else, and she got them the same way anybody does, through stubborn ruthlessness. Joan dreamed the same dreams as everybody else, of fame and luxury. She was simply an exaggerated version of an ordinary person, driven by the same impulses, wishing the same wishes. Joan's sameness was what made her capable of winning the game everybody else was playing.

To someone like Joan Charot, Elsa's fundamental difference was beyond comprehension. *Difference* was what made Elsa capable of achieving things that no ordinary person could possibly imagine. The price of her success was the pain of separation. She lived in a different world from other people, thinking thoughts no one else could think. She was unfathomable to others, and unlovable. The only man who dared to love her had died trying. If he had truly understood her, he might have saved himself from his fate, but she was simply too alien.

He never had a chance. He was right about her, in that she

wasn't working for the good of humanity; there had been times when he knew her better than she knew herself. Yet, he believed that she was simply repeating her mother's mistakes, creating a little clone over whom she had total control. There, he could not have been more wrong. Even she didn't recognize the truth at first; she may have guessed at it once or twice, though it was too humbling to accept. Now, she knew it in her bones. Elsa had found the only way to end her loneliness. Only through her crime could she have met someone as different as herself. Someone different *like* herself. In her ignorance, she had let that being slip away. But now, it was a part of her again. It was inside of her. And once it was born—even if it killed her—she would not die alone.

Elsa stood at the window and waited.

**Early Fred and Ginger design
by Vincenzo Natali**

Early NERD lab designs by Vincenzo Natali

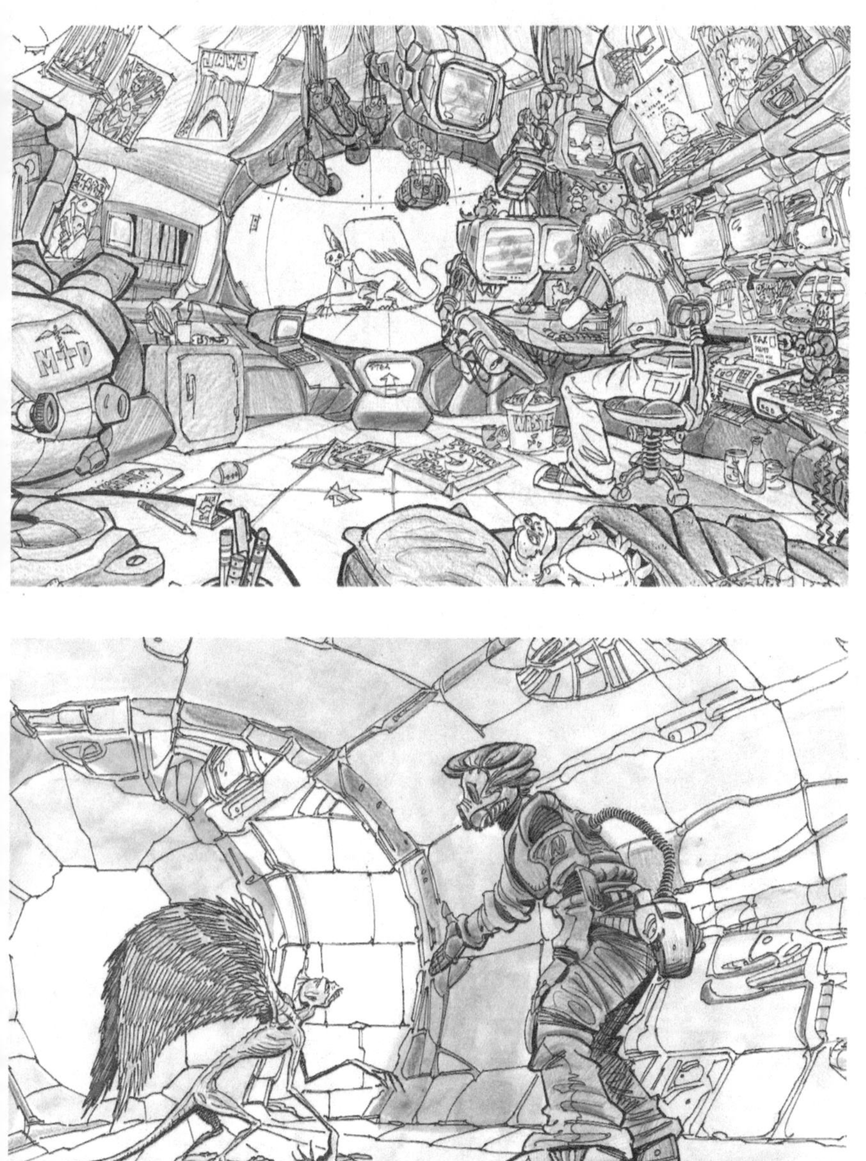

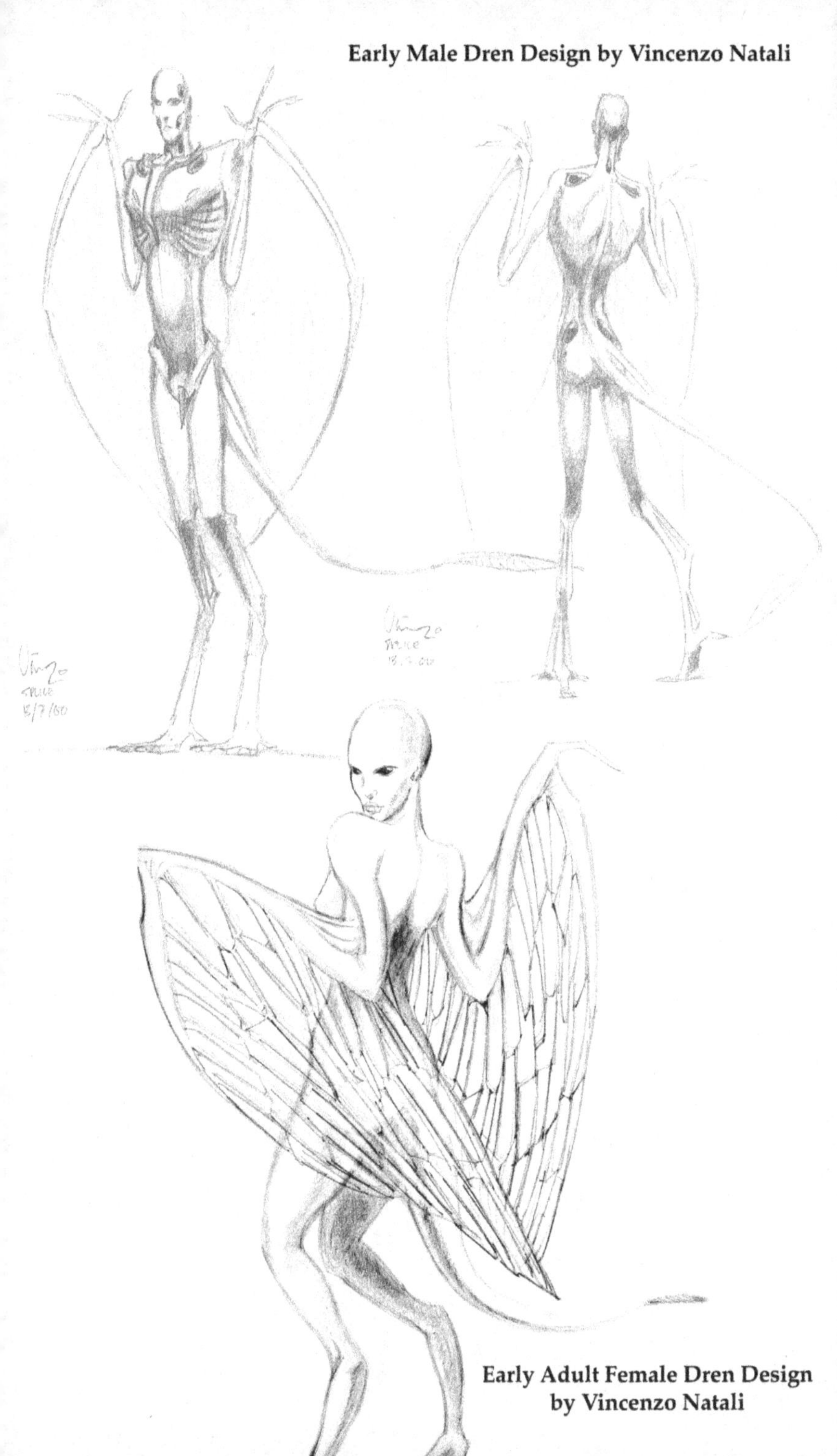

Early Male Dren Design by Vincenzo Natali

**Early Adult Female Dren Design
by Vincenzo Natali**

Early Adult Female Dren Portrait by Vincenzo Natali

Clive and Elsa
by Vincenzo Natali

Love scene storyboards by Vincenzo Natali

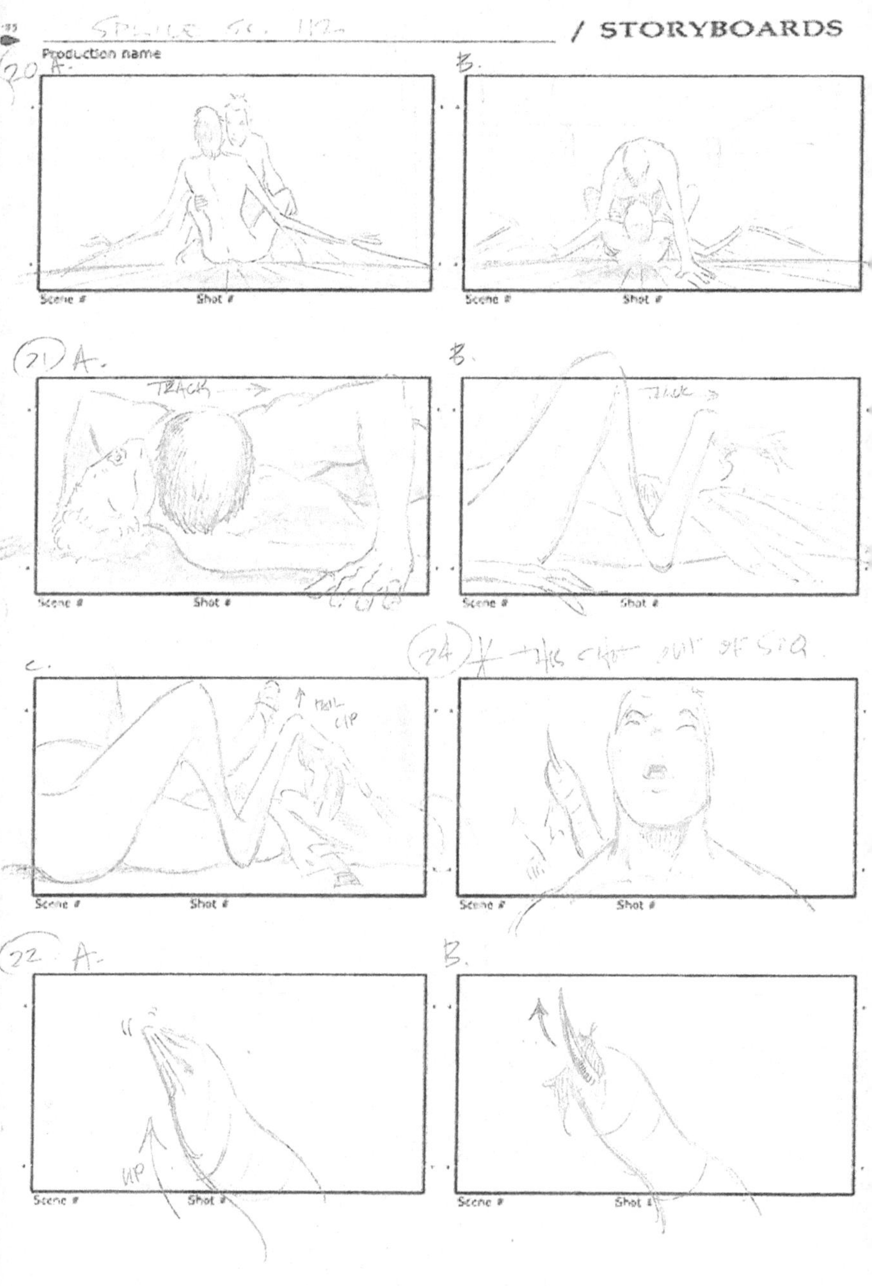

Love scene storyboards by Vincenzo Natali

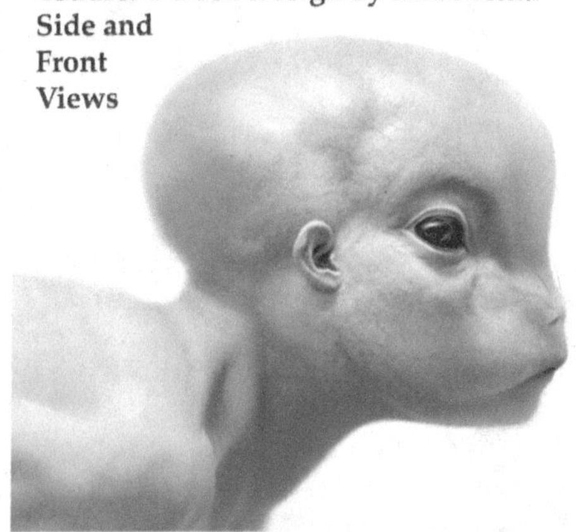

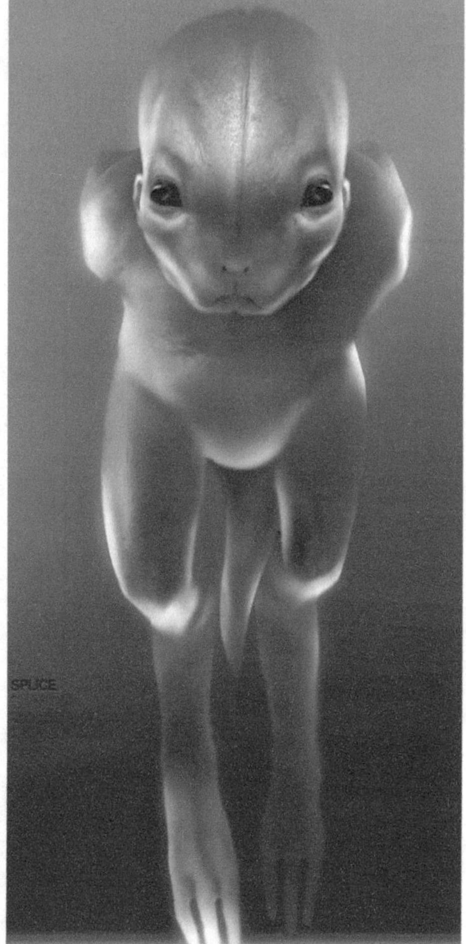

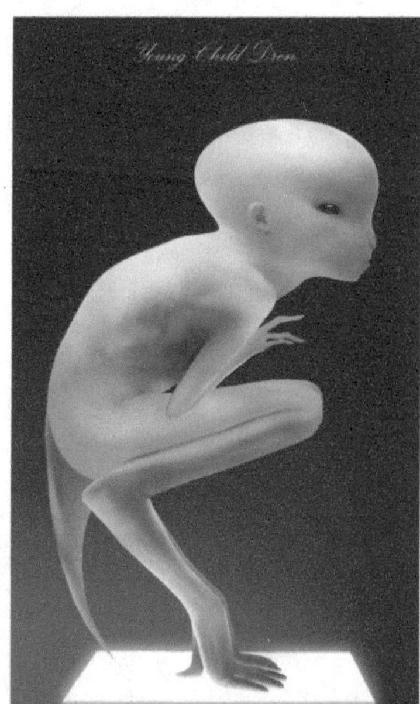

(Above)
Child Dren design
by Peter Konig

Adult Dren Design by Peter Koenig

ACKNOWLEDGMENTS

Without the presence of certain individuals, this strange little project would never have made it out of the incubator. I would like to thank Amy Voorhees Searles for her continued faith and support; Sean Duregger and the Encyclopocalypse team for their trust; my creative partner David Dastmalchian for making me a better writer; Vincenzo Natali for his originality and invaluable encouragement; and my husband David Wolcheck, for letting me be myself.

Claire Donner, December 2023

ABOUT THE AUTHOR

Claire Donner is the Online branch director of the Miskatonic Institute of Horror Studies, programming academic lectures on genre-related subjects for an international audience. Her own research focuses on the blurring of fact and fiction in horror films that are "based on a true story"; she has delivered papers on the Amityville Horror mythos and the film THE ENTITY, and she recorded a commentary track with Miskatonic executive director Josh Saco for the 88 Films release of THE AMITYVILLE HORROR, coming in 2024.

During the summer of 2022, she introduced Michele Soavi's DELLAMORTE DELLAMORE at the Museum of Modern Art for their program "Horror: Messaging the Monstrous", and she subsequently contributed essays to the Severin releases of the Michele Soavi films THE CHURCH, THE SECT, and DELLAMORTE DELLAMORE.

She has served on the jury of the Brooklyn Horror Film Festival, and she writes film criticism in her free time. She lives in Brooklyn, New York with her husband David.